Grind

THE RILEY BROTHERS BOOK 6

E. DAVIES

Publisher's Note: This is a work of fiction. Names, characters, places, and incidents are a product of the author's imagination. Locales and public names are sometimes used for atmospheric purposes. Any resemblance to actual people, living or dead, or to businesses, companies, events, institutions, or locales is completely coincidental.

Grind / E. Davies. – 2nd ed.
ISBN: 978-1-912245-05-5

CHAPTER

One

RYAN

THE ALREADY HALF-BUILT NEIGHBORHOOD LOOKED DIFFERENT every time Ryan drove in after a weekend off. He'd been building here for the last two years. With several streets to go and winter closing in, construction had hit a frenzy.

Even working on the building site, he didn't get a feeling for the progress they were making until he was away. October felt closer now, after Labor Day. A sense of urgency had settled over the building sites again. Everyone knew the ground would freeze quickly. More snow and rain meant having to wrap all their shit up, which was a pain in the ass.

The builders were pushing hard to have all the exteriors finished by the end of October. Then, tradesmen could work inside over the winter. It made sense, but it was shitty timing. Many houses were barely framed on this crescent, which was tucked behind the few remaining trees.

Ryan's apprenticeship last summer had taught him to arrive early. Being the first to the site often meant the boss cornered him for a chat about their upcoming work. At least he usually got coffee out of it.

The site supervisor, Tan, appreciated that Ryan was always on time and didn't skip work. Ryan didn't bevel ultra-precise corners like Roger, and he didn't have delicate fingers for detailed work like Sam, but he was always on time with the right tools.

Hertz's Building had a nondescript site office—a trailer on the empty lot in the middle of the neighborhood. The ground all around was tamped down from the tire tracks of employees' cars and trucks. As he pulled into the lot, noting just a couple of other cars already there, Ryan smiled to himself. There was Tan, in the door of the trailer, holding two coffees.

He parked his truck and climbed out, slamming the door and rounding the hood to approach the trailer. "Morning," he called. "Just couldn't wait for me to get in?"

"I went to bed dreaming of you," Tan answered dryly and rolled his eyes, shoving a coffee at him. Still, he smiled. It wasn't a harsh mockery like some men would make of that line.

Ryan appreciated it. Most of the guys knew about him and were more mature than that, but a few…

"Hope the man measures up to the legend," Ryan smirked. He took the coffee, following Tan into the site office. "How can I improve your life?"

The office was cluttered with paperwork strewn across one desk. Safety notices were pinned to the walls. Tan insisted on keeping the other desk clean except for the work of the day. As Ryan sipped his double-double he made his way over for a look.

Just what he'd expected: finishing the framing for houses 2 through 8, and what looked like a roster. "Oh, you put me with Sam again?"

"You know she needs muscle to hold things while she screws them." To his credit, Tan didn't even start laughing, like many guys would. He just shot Ryan an apologetic glance and shrugged. All the guys knew Ryan wouldn't let anything slide, even accidental comments.

Ryan liked Sam. She was tough and smart, and very good at mental math. He had yet to catch an arithmetic mistake, even though she never used a calculator. He'd found out that she had briefly been an astrophysics major. She'd rarely talked about why she'd ended up here instead. As they were often the only woman and gay man around, Sam and he got along pretty well. They had each other's backs.

"Sure," he agreed. "I'll follow her lead."

Tan rubbed his chin. "There's only a little left to do on each house, but where we lost those four hours Friday…"

Someone had fucked up a lumber order and delivered the wrong load. Nobody had been able to do much all afternoon. By the time the right truck arrived, the guys had just unloaded it before heading home.

Tan had been just about losing his shit, and Ryan didn't blame him. Managing time well was the key to meeting deadlines. As they were building so many houses at once, deadlines were the only way they'd finish before winter.

"We need some overtime this week," Tan admitted. "You interested?"

Ryan usually took it. He had no family ties like some of the guys, and no steady girlfriend like others. In fact, he hadn't dated in months. Not since Isaac had told him he was probably being transferred. He'd disappeared the day after Ryan had said he'd like to make their friends-with-benefits relationship more serious.

Fucking liar. He'd seen him at the co-op a week later.

But Ryan had let it go months ago. He just didn't feel like getting his heart involved with anyone again. And that left him available for overtime, which meant extra money.

"Sure," Ryan agreed and looked over as the door rattled open. It was Ricky, his broad shoulders filling the frame as he edged through at an angle. "Hey, man, how's it going?"

They clapped hands and shook briskly. Ryan held his coffee cup away to keep it from spilling on either of them. Ricky headed over to clap Tan's shoulder. "Great. Good weekend. Ready to get to work."

"Well, someone's an eager beaver," Ryan snorted.

"Had a great date. You should try it sometime."

Ryan rolled his eyes. "Sounds like money down the drain."

"Always a romantic," Ricky laughed. "Tan, where am I today?"

As they settled into their workday, Ryan's mind was still on the Labor Day long weekend. He'd had a barbecue with some of his best friends, then dinner with his parents. He'd finished a few woodworking projects to sell in the business he wanted to start soon. He'd even taken a hike in the wood-lot. Despite it all, something had still been missing.

He had a feeling he knew what it was, but he had no time for that.

No time, and no inclination to put his heart on the line first. That was an expensive mistake.

His mind kept coming back to Ricky's offhanded remark, though, even after work. He grabbed a quick supper and headed out to his garage workshop to finish the wine cabinet he was designing. The words played on his mind.

Maybe I'll sign up for a dating site soon... or something.

With this vague promise to himself, he was able to put it out of mind for the time being. He finished the cut-out scrolls before he headed inside to watch the game.

5

CHAPTER

Two

JAMES

"Two hundred bucks brings it down to... shit, thirty-nine months."

James furrowed his brows as he leaned in closer to the screen, then sighed. His spreadsheet didn't lie, but he didn't like the answer. His credit card interest spreadsheet came with fancy graphs and projections. The only number he cared about—the one that felt the most real—was the *months to pay off* number.

Thirty-nine months.

And that was assuming he didn't have to put anything new on the balance. The interest was killing him, but there was nothing he could do about that now.

Fucking hell. He should move out of this shitty province with its ten percent unemployment rate and seasonal work problem. Since he'd quit his last full-time job, he hadn't been able to find another steady job. Everyone was desperately holding whatever job they had. Even old people couldn't afford to retire from shitty cashier work.

There *were* jobs if you knew people, but his family wasn't from Fredericton. Living closer to them wasn't an option. Just being gay was hard enough in the capital, let alone anywhere else. A gay trans guy? Yeah, he'd escaped to Fredericton the first chance he got, and he wasn't looking back. This was better than his home town, at least.

The only thing he missed from home was the rock-climbing. It was flatter around here, with few good climbing routes. There was an indoor gym, but that wasn't the same as the experience outdoors.

"Let's see." James took a quick glance at his job search spreadsheet. Looked like he hadn't dropped off resumes at the uptown mall in two months. That was just long enough that he should do another round there. Everywhere else he'd tried was too recent and he'd only irritate people by dropping by again.

Except his buddy, Jay, who ran a restaurant downtown. It was worth stopping by to see if they were hiring yet. In the lead-up to Christmas, they sometimes needed extra staff, especially for Christmas parties. James was hoping for at least a temporary position there.

At least his basement apartment downtown was close to a lot of workplaces. If he did get a job at the uptown mall, that would mean an hour on the bus each way. It would only be a stupid fifteen-minute drive at most if he had a damn car.

James couldn't bring himself to regret his decisions, though. He'd done what he had to for survival.

He'd pay for it for years to come, but sooner or later, it would be worth it.

"Jay, hey!"

"Hi, Jay."

They swapped grins. James didn't usually go by that nickname, which he associated too much with his friend. They still joked that they could stand in for each other.

Both of them had the same stereotypical look—short, stubbly, and kind of twinky.

Jay hated it and constantly tried to encourage their beard to grow out into a geeky student look. Being a young restaurant manager was hard enough, let alone one who didn't fit into the gender binary and used "they" pronouns. Jay had managed for a few years now.

But James didn't mind being a pretty boy twink. He could almost grow a beard, even if it was patchy, but he usually didn't need it to be seen as a guy. Either way, it was nice to get attention from guys who didn't think he was a short-haired girl. Drunk straight boys didn't react well when they noticed five-o'clock shadow.

"How's it going?" Jay asked. James waved the stack of papers in his hand, and Jay winced. "Résumés?"

"Yep. So, you know what I'm gonna ask…" James laughed.

They smiled and punched his arm lightly. "You're top of the list, man. Business is too slow still. I'm hoping it'll pick up this month with the students back in town."

James bit back his disappointment. He'd take any job at all, and they knew that. Didn't even have to be a waiter—he'd be a busboy or wash dishes or, hell, clean the floors. Any job with a boss who called him by his real name and didn't look disgusted every time he walked into the break room.

Thank God he'd left his cashier job, even if it had been a fight for employment since. "Looking grossed out and putting me on the cash desk furthest from the door all the time" was hard to prove. The Human Rights Commission here didn't protect the right characteristics, even if he'd wanted to go through the hellish legal system.

"I know," Jay sympathized, catching that disappointed look. Their voice dropped as they stepped closer. "You're still on for the charity auction, though?"

Bits and pieces of work like art auctions for a cause were what James relied on, so of course he was still on. "Yep. Got my best tie pressed," he joked.

They grinned. "Great. Okay, I gotta run and sort out the orders this week." They were scanning his face for signs of real distress. James knew that look—they'd given it to each other before.

James offered a reassuring smile. "Go do your thing. I'm heading up to the mall."

"Good luck," Jay wished him, and leaned in for a quick hug before striding away for their office.

For a moment, James's stomach dropped with envy. He tried not to dwell on it—he was happy when any of his trans siblings did well for themselves. Running a business in a climate like this was hard. But there was a natural envy, too, that he hadn't been able to do that yet.

James had a business degree, which was only useful for helping others with their business plans, and a can-do attitude. He had no specialized skills to market and sell. He wrote articles online and cut lawns, but those were things any kid could do.

Sometimes it felt like he'd missed all his adolescent years. He was just getting around to restarting them now. He'd wasted so much time in limbo, waiting to grow into the man he needed to be.

Things could be worse, though. They could always be worse.

He plugged his headphones into his iPhone as he headed for the bus stop, preparing for the long bus ride. One of these days, he'd get ahead.

CHAPTER
Three

RYAN

As Noah ran a fingertip over the little wooden ring box, his eyes widened and smile grew. Ryan's chest swelled with pride. The finer details on it had been damn hard, especially for a guy like him. He was used to working with two-by-sixes, not two-inch cubes of wood.

He'd taken his sweet time, working over the course of a few months to try different designs for his good friend. They'd finally found a box design they both liked. Then it had been a trial of different woods and designs, and the process of actually building it.

"Wow," Noah whispered. "It's incredible. And so detailed."

"God, I'm never doing a damn ring box again," Ryan grumbled. Holding a screwdriver between his thumb and forefinger for the tiny screws of the tiny fucking hinges? No, thanks.

Noah laughed as he turned it this way and that. He played with the golden clasp and unlatched it. As he opened the box, he caught his breath. Ryan had put the smooth, velvet-covered foam inside with a slit cut in it for the ring.

It was always easy to read Noah's emotions. The spirited blond was vocal about his reactions, whether positive or negative, so the glowing praise meant a lot to Ryan. Ryan tended to be quiet, but Noah talked more, so they balanced each other out.

"Thinking about the proposal?" Ryan asked after a few moments of watching Noah's shifting expressions.

Noah touched his forehead and nodded, his gaze on the box before he flipped it shut again and drew a breath. "Yeah. It's big."

"Of course it is." Ryan hadn't known him as long as he'd known Cam, Noah's soon-to-be fiancé, but anyone could tell that they were perfect for each other. They couldn't get enough of each other. Didn't mean Noah wouldn't get a case of nerves first.

Ryan shifted nervously, hoping he wasn't going to be expected to play counselor here. He could build them a wedding bed given enough time and instructions, but helping them get there? Nuh uh. That was up to their other friends—Thomas, soft-spoken and kind; Chase, intense and fiercely loyal; even Kevin, loud-mouthed but honest enough to tell you if you were marrying the right man.

"God, you look like I'm asking you to walk through coals," Noah laughed as he dug his wallet out. "Don't worry."

"No, I..." Ryan trailed off, his cheeks flushing. He didn't want Noah to think he didn't care, because he did. He just didn't know how to handle feelings as well as some.

Noah winked and handed over a wad of cash. "Don't worry about it. Here you go."

"Is there a tip in here?" Ryan accused, squinting at the thicker-than-expected stack of green.

Though Noah playfully shrugged, his answering grin told Ryan that he was right. "If there is, it's well-earned."

Ryan sighed but pocketed it, then half-hugged him. "Enjoy."

"I will." Noah carefully placed the box into his desk drawer, his gaze lingering on the drawer even after he shut it.

Ryan had met him at the art gallery where he worked as a curator. That way, Noah could hide the ring until he found a good hiding spot at home. He'd never actually been into Noah's place of work before now, but it made perfect sense for him. He had art pieces scattered around the office, photos of himself and Cam—and their whole group.

Wait a second, that photo's from our barbecue last weekend!

"You were quick!" Ryan laughed, pointing out that framed photo on the desk. "How sentimental. Had to make sure you had us all on your desk?" Noah was part of the glue that held their friendship group together. Ryan wasn't missing the chance to tease him.

Noah grinned, unashamed. "A man who tries at least half a dozen times to burn the perfect bee into my wedding ring box, and gives me a choice of bees? That's not sentimental at all."

That was just good customer service. Ryan snorted but let him have that one, turning his back to head for the doorway of his office.

Noah laughed behind him. "But seriously, our last group photo didn't have Matty, so…"

It was another stark reminder that Ryan was the odd one out in their group of friends—Cam, Jackson, and Thomas, the brothers at the heart of it, and their boyfriends Noah, Chase, and Alex respectively, plus Floyd and Greyson, and now Kevin and Matty. Other friends had come and gone, but they were all still close.

And Ryan was the sad single one. The last girl standing up against the gym wall.

The mental image of himself waiting to be picked at the dance, all muscles and shy glances, made Ryan chuckle under his breath. That had never been his scene anyway.

Noah was watching him with a much-too-perceptive expression on his face for Ryan's comfort. They strode down the hall of the art gallery toward the exit. The charity art auction that Noah was curating tonight was next door, at a restaurant. Ryan was attending, along with a couple of their friends.

"Don't give me that pitying look," Ryan rolled his eyes. "I'm fine."

"I'm not pitying you," Noah piped up, laughing. "But I can work on setting up a blind date…"

Ryan flicked his shoulder. He didn't dare shove him around like he might Jackson, the blacksmith with arms bigger than Ryan's. Noah might go through the wall. "Don't."

"I'm just saying!"

Ryan shook his head. "I'd rather get my business off the ground first. I'll have time for… love… later." As soon as the word slipped out of his mouth, he almost groaned.

"Love," Noah repeated, his expression lighting up gleefully. "See? Romantic. Just say the word, I'll see who knows someone you might like."

Ryan held the art gallery door and shook his head, following Noah to the restaurant.

He didn't *need* a boyfriend, and besides, love didn't work like that. It didn't have a schedule or convenient timing. No doubt he'd stumble into it at exactly the wrong moment.

Ryan didn't doubt that it was just Noah's teasing that was on his mind. That was the only reason he looked twice at the guy behind Jay, adjusting the number tags on the art pieces.

He was cute. Short, dark-haired, stubbled, with beautiful brown eyes.

Nothing said he was gay, but Ryan had a feeling, and he was rarely wrong. His gaydar was pretty accurate. Even if the guy was dressed like all the other event staff, there was something… tidy about him.

"Who's that?" he asked Noah, nodding toward him. "I didn't see him last time."

"Oh, that's one of Jay's buddies," Noah said. To his credit, he didn't give Ryan an obnoxious grade-school smirk while he did it. His lips were quivering in a smile, though. "Pretty sure he's gay, since that's what you're asking. Don't know if he's single…"

"Thanks, Detective. Should I just start calling you Detective Riley now?"

"Shh," Noah hissed and slapped his arm harder than Ryan expected.

Ryan jumped, then laughed and held up his hands. He wasn't going to give away Noah's secret. "Sorry, sorry. You better hurry up and do it, though," he teased. "In case you get cold feet."

Noah was only half-listening to him now, his eyes on the other side of the room. Ryan rolled his eyes. He already knew who he'd find there, and sure enough, when he looked over, it was Cam.

And Cam was giving Noah the same gooey eyes.

Fucking hell. Of all the guys, they'd been the first two to

get together, but they were still the sappiest around each other. If this was what love did to a person, he was fine tinkering around in his garage.

Ryan wandered off for snacks, and, as expected, Noah barely seemed to notice him leave. He was too busy hugging Cam and murmuring to him, both of them smiling at each other.

Exasperation made Ryan's stomach clench, not jealousy.

"I should tell my curator he's not allowed to invite his boyfriend." That was Jay, laughing behind Ryan. Ryan had to look down by his shoulder to find the much shorter person. He stepped back so Jay didn't have to strain their neck. "Every time he comes with him, I have to pry the two of them apart."

"I think it's a buy one, get one free deal," Ryan smiled. "Besides, more eye candy to attract the buyers."

Having good-looking men around, even if they were gay couples, drew some women to these auctions. Noah and Cam were a fixture, and not just because Cam had been a hockey player before his heart problem. Now, Cam worked for Noah's uncle, who was a beekeeper. People had rallied around Cam when he traveled out to Ontario for his medical diagnosis and treatment last year. They hadn't forgotten him afterward. He'd almost been famous; they could overlook the gay thing for that.

There were *some* good things about a town this size.

Ryan's gaze was drawn back to the new assistant. "I don't think he's been at the last couple auctions?" He phrased it as a question to Jay.

"That's James. I want to hire him next, whenever business picks up again enough that I can."

Ryan winced. Even as a prospective business owner, he

could empathize with that. "I get that. That's why my carpentry thing's been on hold," he told Jay, folding his arms and frowning. "I need someone to do all the non-carpentry stuff: marketing, sales, networking," he explained while Jay nodded. "But I couldn't pay someone yet. It's a catch-22."

"Right. You're serious about starting this up?" Jay asked.

Ryan nodded.

"Well, there's grants, and the small business development group that can help you." Jay was in business mode now. "Do you have a business plan?"

"Sort of. I filled one out from the internet." Ryan had almost forgotten about it. Working dawn 'till dusk all summer on building sites had sapped his energy to pick it back up and finish it. "But I have to finish that first, I guess."

"You can approach the council and they'll help you finish it."

The voice near his elbow was warm and crackly, and a shiver ran straight down Ryan's spine. He didn't have to turn to know that it was James, but he did anyway, smiling warmly.

James was smiling back, nodding at Jay. "Sorry, couldn't help overhearing. But so many people don't realize that you don't have to have *everything* together to approach an incubator."

"You worked at the one on campus, didn't you?" Jay asked.

James nodded, his dark hair flopping into his eyes.

"Ohhh." Ryan shifted, turning more toward James. "So I'm talking to an expert."

James looked flustered, but he grinned up at him. "Sure, I'll take the compliment." God, he was short—had to be five-foot-seven? Six? A good five or six inches shorter, just short enough that he'd tuck under Ryan's chin...

Nope. This is professional.

Ryan clearly needed to get laid before he started thinking that way about *every* new guy he met.

"He's got a head for business," Jay spoke up. "I'll leave you two to it. We've got ten minutes before the auction starts," Jay told James. They walked off to talk to a couple of newcomers.

That left the two of them alone, and Ryan tried to ignore the nervous tingles that crawled down his spine.

"I'm James, by the way," the cute guy introduced himself, holding out a hand.

Ryan's hand dwarfed James's as he took it. "Ryan." The moment their palms touched, an extra nervous tingle crawled down Ryan's spine. He nodded. "Good to meet you."

"You, too." James took a step back, propping a hand on his hip. "So you have a business plan almost done?"

"Maybe half-done," Ryan admitted with an embarrassed laugh. "I got confused and kind of stopped. It's hard to budget when I don't know what my sales projections would be."

"Right. You haven't done market research?"

Ryan sighed and shook his head. "No time, over the summer. Really, I'd be happy with more of a side business. Sell a few things a week. But with overtime on job sites..."

"You work in the trades?" James glanced down at his forearms, his gaze trailing up Ryan's strong forearms and biceps back up to his face. "That explains..." His cheeks turned crimson.

"My size?" Ryan teased, the knot in his stomach uncoiling. James looked like fun to tease. "Lift shit all day and you, too, can have trouble finding shirt sleeves that fit."

"Oh, that sounds like a first-world problem," James scoffed. "I'm so sorry. Meanwhile, I have trouble opening jars."

Ryan burst out laughing. "Call me, I'll break the jar or open it."

"No way."

"It was a weak jar," Ryan defended himself. His chest swelled anyway at the impressed look James gave him. It was nice to be admired sometimes, even if it wasn't going to go anywhere.

Strictly professional, right? James was interested in his business, not him.

James confirmed his suspicion a moment later by breaking the gaze, looking back to the art pieces. "I'd better get back to work. If you wanna swap numbers, I'll look over your plan and get you unstuck."

"That'd be great," Ryan admitted, grabbing his phone to enter James's number. If nothing else, a friend to help nudge him into starting to pursue his dream would be nice.

Four

JAMES

It was impossible to miss the man who walked in the door. Not Noah, a guy James sort of knew from bumping into him in passing at the restaurant, but the man next to him.

He was tall, broad-shouldered, but lean and muscled. James could tell at a glance that he wasn't the kind of guy who kissed his own biceps good night. Though he wore trousers and a dress shirt, he looked like he'd be more comfortable in jeans.

Definitely the kind of guy who tinkered with engines or built bridges or something manly as fuck.

James's first instinct was usually to be intimidated by that kind of guy. The newcomer was also good-looking as hell, though. It made James want to catch his eye and see… Well, just see.

He worked his way around the edge of the room, fidgeting with number tags, until he was close enough to listen in. James had to make sure this was one of Jay's gay friends. It could be some poor straight guy, roped into coming along, who'd run from a pretty little guy batting his lashes at him.

His interest shifted from personal to professional when he overheard them talking business, though. This was the one thing he knew enough about to interrupt—and in fact, he couldn't help himself. He didn't want misconceptions to keep *anyone* from starting a business. That went double for someone in his own community.

The moment they met, it was pretty clear that Ryan was interested in his business knowledge. James managed to fumble his way through the conversation without outright ogling him. Having Ryan's full attention on him was almost overwhelming. God, those pretty brown eyes.

James was glad for the excuse to make his way behind the tables again and start reading through the auction sheets. The work caught him up as he moved from piece to piece. It was his job to note the bids and handle the payment while Jay announced auction winners.

Cute or not, James forgot about Ryan for the next two hours. He moved from painting to painting, making conversation with the buyers. He had to make them feel good about their donations. Repeat buyers were like gold.

Forgot about Ryan, that was, until he got to one piece, a small painting of a bee sitting on a flower petal. He listened for the name Jay called out, which was *Ryan Hart,* and then the very same Ryan walked up.

Suddenly, James wasn't in smooth "make conversation and ask for the payment method" mode. He stumbled over his words.

"Great job bidding and… choosing," James smiled when Ryan reached him. "Ryan Hart, right? Is that H-A-R-T?"

Ryan's deep voice rumbled again, sending a shiver down James's spine. "Yes, it is. Thanks. It's not for me, actually."

"Oh?" James's heart sank for a second, but he kept smiling. *Don't let it be for a boyfriend.*

"A couple friends…" Ryan leaned in. James instinctively met him halfway, leaning across the table.

He smelled like spice and pine. Oh, fuck, he smelled *good*.

"Are getting engaged," Ryan murmured. His voice was low under the crowd's babble and Jay's banter about the next piece.

"Oh. Surprise?"

"Yes. The proposal hasn't happened yet," Ryan murmured, and his gaze flicked back to Noah.

It took James a couple of seconds to clue in. "*Oh.* Oh, cool."

He'd seen Noah hanging around the guy he assumed was his boyfriend in the breaks between auctions. He was a hunky dude with a sweet smile and a crooked nose.

Ryan winked and straightened up again. "I'll save it for the wedding. Pretty sure I'll only have to store it for a couple months."

James laughed as he took Ryan's credit card to swipe. "You think?"

"Mmm. They're that type, yeah. I'd better get my suit ready," Ryan joked.

James chuckled. "There, thank you. Do you want to pick it up later or take it home tonight?"

Then, Ryan's gaze flickered up and down James's body, taking in his tie and vest and tight jeans. James's heart caught in his throat. His body prickled with pleasant heat. If Ryan took advantage of that line, he was not going to say no.

Unfortunately, Ryan just gave an easy smile and nodded. "I'll take it, yeah."

James swallowed hard. *Not everyone wants you,* he reminded himself. "Cool." New friends were fine, too. "So I'll get in touch about the business plan, if you want?"

"Yes, please," Ryan nodded. "I'll take you for coffee if that's a fair trade."

"Fair enough," James agreed. Jay was announcing the next piece, and he had to move on. "Thanks for your purchase. Our charities appreciate it."

After his standard line, Ryan melted back into the crowd and James tried to get back into the zone. Swipe the card, joke around, thank them, move on, help Jay get through these last dozen pieces before they ran over time.

He couldn't spare the time to fantasize about burly carpenters sweeping him off his feet.

CHAPTER

Five

RYAN

The chilly autumn breeze rustled at Ryan's back as he pushed open the door to the coffee shop.

He'd promised to meet James here. After a long damn Tuesday, it was a welcome break for him, and James had sounded excited in his text messages.

Ryan worried he'd sound like an idiot, but James had helped entrepreneurs with much vaguer ideas.

And, to be honest, Ryan was looking forward to some time spent with another guy, one-on-one. Hanging out with all his friends was fun, but it was exhausting sometimes. And not just in the "everyone else has a boyfriend-or-soon-fiancé" way. The atmosphere around them tended to be high-energy.

He hoped he didn't come off as a quiet weirdo to James. *Talk about yourself, just keep it real,* he reminded himself as he looked around the shop.

It was easy to spot James in the corner once he looked past the discarded pile of layers: coat, sweater, scarf, and gloves.

"On your way to the North Pole?" Ryan teased, grinning as he unzipped his jacket and dumped it on the opposite side of the booth from James.

James rose to his feet and laughed. He was so much shorter that he had to crane his neck back. "I get cold easily. Shut up."

Ryan's eyes still twinkled with amusement, but he let James get away without more teasing. "What do you want? I'm buying."

An odd expression—relief?—passed across James's face, and then he nodded. "Thanks."

"Least I can do. You won't be thanking me once you see my paperwork," Ryan laughed.

James waved it off and stood up to go with him to the counter. "Small mocha soy cappuccino, please."

Ryan nodded, skimming the board for something he wanted to drink. "Something to eat?"

James hesitated but forged ahead. "Blueberry bagel, please. With hummus."

"Hummus?" Ryan questioned. He knew it was tasty on falafel wraps—a couple of coworkers had brought him out for falafel for lunch before. He didn't make a habit of eating the stuff, though. It didn't sound appetizing on a bagel, in the morning.

"It's good for you, and full of protein," James defended himself with a laugh. "Why, are you going for a Meaty McCheese snack?"

"The sausage and egg muffin."

"Gross," James teased. "All those fats first thing in the morning?"

"It's only the trans ones you have to watch out for," Ryan countered.

James burst out laughing, and Ryan stared at him for a moment. James covered his mouth, muted chuckles still escaping. "Sorry. Yeah." He was bouncing on his toes, his eyes sparkling.

Ryan liked the energy that seemed to be sizzling under his skin. He was a lively one, and better yet, James kept grinning at him like they were in on a shared secret.

Ryan recited their order of drinks and food—he took a double-double coffee with the gross sandwich he intended to fully enjoy.

"So you're vegetarian? Vegan?" Ryan asked when they moved to the pickup side of the counter.

James chuckled. "Something like that."

"Why? Health?"

"A bit of this, a bit of that. I'll sometimes cave on my mom's neighbors' eggs—they have chickens. But meat's right out. And dairy..." James shuddered.

"Not even cheese? How do you survive?"

James looked mischievous as he leaned up toward Ryan, his voice low. "Vegans taste better."

Ryan didn't know what to say that, except to laugh and try *not* to picture James squirming on the bed under him. James was cute as *hell*, but that didn't mean he was going to fuck him. No matter how much the heat tingled down his spine every time he brushed against James's arm.

"You're redder than the ketchup on your gross snack choice," James teased.

Another laugh bubbled from Ryan as he shook his head. James was one of those cute, wicked smart boys Ryan had always admired from afar. He wasn't sure he could keep up with his witty tongue, but he'd love to try. "Are you dating anyone?" Ryan asked, before he thought about it. Then, he realized how inappropriate that could be. "I, um, if you want to say," he added.

A startled laugh escaped James as he shook his head. "I don't mind. Nah, I'm not. You?"

"Nope," Ryan said simply.

There was a moment of silence between them as Ryan's eyes met James's beautiful brown ones. Then, they both spoke at once.

"The last guy—"

"I'm not—"

Ryan gestured for James to keep going.

"The last guy was a jerk, in retrospect. I haven't dated steadily since," James finished. "Ugh, guys."

"Tell me about it," Ryan smiled. "Late last year, my sort-of-boyfriend pretended to transfer out of town. I'm not really looking right now."

James looked offended on his behalf, recoiling and shaking his head with a slight gasp. "What a dick."

Ryan shrugged, though he appreciated the sympathy. He picked up the coffee cups when the barista delivered them. "I'll bring these back to the table."

"Sure."

When James joined him at the table, he pushed Ryan's plate as far away from him as he could. He playfully put the napkin holder between them with a flick of his wrist. "That's better."

Another laugh bubbled from Ryan's chest. He sipped his coffee, gazing across the table at James for a second. It was easy talking to him. His face was an open book. "So, do you work for Jay?"

"Just odd jobs for now," James told him. "They call me for events and stuff. They said they want to hire me when business picks up, but you know. This economy and all."

Ryan nodded. He didn't know Jay well—Noah and Chase talked about them a lot, but they didn't tend to hang out together. Still, they seemed all right. It had taken Ryan a while to learn their pronouns, so he'd awkwardly avoided them when talking to Noah or Chase until he was sure he'd get it right. "They seem like a good boss. You're looking for a job?"

"I'm always applying for jobs," James grimaced. "Someday. What about you?"

"Carpentry. Finished my apprenticeship last year. I build houses on the north side."

"Oh, you're responsible for all that suburban growth," James grinned. "That sounds like tough work. Do the guys you work with... know about you?"

Ryan might have rebuffed the question, but James looked curious and open. Somehow, he didn't mind talking about this shit with the guy, even though he barely knew him. "Most of them. Of them, most of them are okay with it."

"There's always some, though," James muttered.

Ryan nodded, letting silence fall for a few moments.

"That's why I quit my last job, at a grocery store. I could have pursued legal action, but..." James shrugged, putting down his cup in favor of the bagel. "Whatever," he said around a mouthful.

Ryan nodded, finishing his sandwich. He understood the desire to just be done with it. "Sorry."

"No, it's fine. I'm glad to be out of there. New chapter and all." Still, there were stress lines around James's eyes as he smiled. Ryan's gaze lingered on them for a few moments. James caught his eyes, licking the hummus off his fingers as he finished his bagel. His tongue circled his fingertips, and he wasn't looking away.

Ryan knew he was blushing again. He grabbed napkins to wipe his hands off, then rummaged in his bag for papers, refusing to look up again for a few seconds. When he did, James was smirking, but mercifully, he didn't say anything. "So, uh, my business plans… woodworking."

"Right."

"I want to start a woodworking business. Standard farmer's market thing," Ryan told him. "Friends and family are always buying things. They said I should sell to the public, not just friends of friends."

James's eyes lit up. "Yes. That's a great opportunity. And you clearly have the skills. You're not considering doing custom work?"

"Not until I have a few years' more experience. I still learn every day on the job," Ryan told him. It wasn't a blow to his pride to say so—just a matter-of-fact admission. "But I've been building things since workshop class in high school. I feel more confident doing that. Besides, I don't have the time to work on custom projects. This kind of stuff, I can pick up and put down."

James was nodding, leaning back with one hand wrapped around the cup. The other arm was folded across himself.

The ache was itching in Ryan's muscles after the work day. He shifted and rolled his shoulders to keep it from settling in just yet. It was a familiar, bone-deep exhaustion. He'd used it as an excuse for the last year as to why he hadn't already started his business.

"What do you need?" James asked.

That was an interesting question. Ryan blinked for a second, startled, then thoughtful. "I need… someone to handle the business side of things. I can make things. It's everything else I don't have time and energy for. My brother and some of my friends keep suggesting I hire someone or partner with someone. I've never found someone with enough of a head for business and the free time. Once the expenses are paid off, a fifty-fifty profit split."

Already, an idea was tingling at the back of his mind. He tilted his head as he watched James.

"Right," James agreed, nodding. "So, let's see your business plan and anything else you've got drawn up."

Ryan slid his paperwork across the table, focusing on drinking his coffee while James looked everything over. His cheeks were hot with embarrassment. Waiting for a conclusion was hard, but he didn't interrupt James.

At last, James nodded to himself and looked up. "This isn't bad. Aside from the lack of any financial data at all," he teased, grinning up at Ryan again as he settled back.

"I know, I know…" Ryan laughed. "I just didn't know how to do sales projections."

"I'm guessing you haven't done a lot of pricing research."

"Well, I know what I charge friends and family—usually materials plus labor. I know I'm supposed to charge more," Ryan explained. "And I know how much people charge for the usual tacky Christmas decorations at markets and stuff. I never sat down and decided what to make, and how many of them and when…"

James was nodding. "Gotcha. Okay…" He was scribbling notes on Ryan's papers.

God, that was cute handwriting. It suited him perfectly.

Financial projections—market research.

Ryan felt like he was undergoing an interview. James asked him more questions about everything he'd written, scribbling clarifications down. It was more and more impressive, though.

"And farmers' markets would be your primary sales outlet?"

"At first, I'm thinking," Ryan nodded. "If I can get in."

"Right. One of them is easier to get into as a new vendor," James told him. "The main market, not so much."

"Oh," Ryan frowned. "Really? Cam works there."

"Mhmm, because his boyfriend's uncle has been around for years. Are there other honey vendors?"

"No…" Ryan furrowed his brows.

"Because they limit competition. All markets do, to some extent. Or they could wind up with a room full of soap makers and nothing else. The application process is easy, though…"

"Right." Ryan took mental notes, but James was quickly losing him as he explained who to get in touch with and what paperwork he needed.

He must have been frowning, because James stopped. "Sorry. I can write that down for you."

"Actually," Ryan spoke up tentatively, bracing his fore-arms on the table. His coffee was cold now, long forgotten in favor of talking to this cute young guy who happened to be a wealth of business knowledge. "I had another idea. You don't have a job and you need one… I don't have time, but I need someone to run this…"

It was impossible for James to hide the hopeful spark in his eye. He looked up at Ryan, his pen poised over paper and tongue stuck out between his teeth.

Ryan bit back his smile and raised his brows. "If you're interested, of course."

"Wait, you'd want to work with me?" James looked stunned. "Are you sure?"

"I'm positive." Being more of a listener than a talker gave Ryan certain advantages. He could read people pretty well. He could often tell who was an asshole and who was worth listening to and hanging out with. James seemed honest, hard-working, and clever. That was enough to get by with.

Besides, working with anyone on this would be better than doing nothing, like he had for the last year.

"Wow. Well, um." James fidgeted, his face clouding over for a moment as he looked down at the papers, clicking the pen.

"You don't have to—" Ryan started. What if this wasn't up James's alley after all?

"I want to," James interrupted, licking his lips. "You should just know, some people in town are kinda weird about me."

A guy as cute and charming as him? Yeah, he looked pretty openly gay, but Ryan was sure as fuck not holding that against him. He didn't want business from assholes who wouldn't buy from him if they knew about him, either.

"In a homophobic way?"

"And transphobic." James's face was tense, his shoulders stiff as he watched Ryan's reactions. Suddenly, Ryan was self-conscious of his reaction, which was confusion at first.

It took Ryan a second to put the pieces together. After all, he'd met—and dated—short guys with high-pitched voices before. Just to be sure, Ryan had to ask, and he spoke slowly, trying to find the best way to put it. "You're a guy now, right?"

"Compliment accepted," James responded, his face cracking into another little smile. "Yeah. *Assigned at birth* is the phrase you're looking for," he teased, his eyes gleaming. "But I was assigned female at birth." He was smiling crookedly but he was still tense, like he was waiting for the other shoe to drop.

Ryan relaxed and chuckled, committing that phrase to memory. "Sorry," Ryan added with a quick laugh. "I mean, I know Jay, but I've never met… or at least never knew I've met… trans guys. Only trans women, and I'm gay, so I don't date them, you know?"

"There's more of us around than you think," James chuckled. He was slowly relaxing, his smiles more genuine again. "But yeah, that's why I left my last job. They wouldn't stop deadnaming me—calling me by my birth name," he explained before Ryan could ask. "And generally being assholes."

"Shit." Ryan frowned and shook his head. This wasn't exactly the most progressive place to live. It was getting better, but it was disappointing nonetheless. "Sorry."

"No need," James assured him. "But now I've got my name changed, at least, so I can apply for jobs. But then there's references, and my SIN number… And I can't update my birth certificate, either."

Ryan had never thought about that. He winced as the implications sank in. "So it's kind of like starting afresh."

"Exactly."

"That's bullshit."

James laughed, maybe at Ryan's straightforward bluntness. "Yeah. So if I'm selling on your behalf… some people will be weird."

"Fuck 'em," Ryan shook his head. "You're cute and engaging. You worked the crowds well at the auction. That's all I care about. Some people don't like me, either." He shrugged.

This time, it was James who blushed, the pink crawling

up his neck to his cheeks as he rubbed at the stubble on his jaw. And somehow, he was just as cute as he had been five minutes ago, before he'd told Ryan.

For the hundredth time, Ryan dragged his mind off James's cute smile. *You're about to go into business with the guy. Dating him would be the worst possible idea.* He might not know much about entrepreneurship, but he knew *that* much.

"Thanks," James laughed. "So, I know some good lawyers. They can draw up a quick letter of intent rather than a contract. It tends to be cheaper and more flexible while we work out this phase of the business."

Shit, he knew his stuff.

"We'll work it out so you just handle manufacturing, and I work on the public face of the business. There'll be a lot more work upfront to build inventory and get the business set up." James narrowed his eyes, drumming his fingers. "If we move fast, we'll be ready for Christmas markets."

Christmas? Ryan stared. "It's only September!"

James laughed and shook his head. "I'm guessing you don't go to a lot of them. They start very soon. By October, they're in full swing."

"Oh. Shit." Ryan had never taken good note of the dates.

"Yep. What's your work schedule like this week?" James asked, digging out his phone to flip through his calendar. "I need to see your workshop and get some spreadsheets set up. And this week, and weekend, I'll look at pricing. I'll need to talk to you about material costs."

James's brain was working fifty to the dozen. "Take a look." Ryan opened his calendar app and passed over his own phone. James looked back and forth between the phones as he talked.

In minutes, he had his work schedule cut out for him:

James was coming to his workshop that weekend. Then, he had to work at least an hour per day in the workshop. He found himself promising not to take on extra overtime and wear himself out, and to get proper sleep and nutrition.

He couldn't help but laugh. "Are you my life coach, too?"

"I've just seen a lot of worn-out entrepreneurs," James told him as he passed back his phone. "The first couple years are the hardest."

"Right."

Somehow, in these couple hours, he'd gone from idly looking at business ideas to setting one up, but... it felt right. And James felt like the right person to do it with.

Ryan's heart was light as he reached across the table, offering James a hand. James looked at it for a second like he didn't know what to do with it.

"To our new business," Ryan told him.

Then, James's face lit up and he gripped Ryan's hand, his palm disappearing into Ryan's but his grip firm as they shook hands.

"Our new business. Congratulations, you new entrepreneur."

What the hell have I done?

Then, James let go and resumed typing notes into his phone, murmuring under his breath. "Material costs... get in touch with the grant people... website... see if Harry's here this weekend about a letter of intent." Ryan pushed away his disappointment when James started to shrug on his jacket. It was getting late, anyway, and Ryan had to get home and eat a proper supper.

"Okay, that's all for you," James directed him. "I've got my work cut out for me this week. I'll text you updates."

"Perfect." Ryan's heart soared with appreciation for

everything James was taking on board as easily as that. He had the feeling he wasn't going to be the boss here, but he was fine with that.

They both rose to their feet, and James nodded at Ryan. "I'll see you at the workshop on Saturday. I put reminders into your phone. I'll take your paperwork and fix it up."

"Okay," Ryan laughed, waiting until James was bundled up with the folder of papers under his arm. Then, he leaned in for a quick one-armed hug. "Thanks a lot, man."

James beamed back at him, clapping his back before he let go and offered a fist bump. "No, thank you."

Ryan bumped their fists together with a laugh, then raised his hand in a quick wave.

His buddies had been bugging him for months to get going on this. He'd made excuses—no time, no energy, more paperwork needed. Maybe all he needed, this whole time, was a James to kick his ass into gear.

Ryan usually didn't believe in fate, but their meeting seemed like the perfect coincidence.

CHAPTER

Six

JAMES

"AHA!"

James pulled out the plaid shirt at the back of his closet, shoving the other hangers out of the way. He tried to avoid buying plaid, but he was a New Brunswicker, after all. Winter called for insulated plaid sweaters. Of course he had *some* plaid hiding at the back of his closet.

He looked so Canadian it almost hurt, but he laughed as he pulled on the red plaid shirt and tucked it into his dark jeans. Now he was dressed to meet his new business partner at the workshop.

The whole week seemed surreal. Once he got over the initial surprise, Ryan hadn't seemed fazed when James had come out to him.

James smiled as he combed his hair and brushed his teeth, glancing at himself in the mirror. These days, a lot of people had at least a basic understanding what he meant when he came out to them. And aside from a little verbal fumbling, Ryan had handled it well.

It was easy to tell who started looking for the girl they

were sure was hidden within him, like he was trying to trick them. Others might not know the language but got the idea. Ryan, even if he'd been embarrassed by his ignorance, was in the latter group, which was a huge relief. Hot guys never seemed to get it.

Not that he cared how hot Ryan was. They were working together now, after all.

But with that out of the way, James had been happy to sign on as business partners. His lawyer friend was working on a letter of intent for them. James had been researching local woodworking businesses all week, up to this morning at the farmer's markets.

Both of them. Even if he'd had to take the bus to the north side market, which was a huge pain in the ass.

God, James needed a car, but thinking about his credit made James wince. It was motivation to get this business off the ground for both of their sakes.

And now he was off for a brisk walk to Ryan's house, which was about half an hour by foot. He sometimes biked around town if the walk would be any longer. This was just close enough that he didn't mind.

This time of year, the walk *was* brisk, but it didn't freeze his face and hands off, at least. Soon, he'd have to switch to buses again. Getting around in winter was a lot harder than the summer because of all the damn snow.

Still, by the time he reached Ryan's house—a little bungalow with a garage almost the same size as the house, set back on the lot—his lips were numb. He had his hands shoved into his pockets. For all Ryan teased him, James wouldn't dare go out without a scarf and gloves from now until Canada Day.

It was easy to tell where Ryan was—just approaching the

door, he could hear soft thuds. He knocked, and seconds later, he heard, "Come in!"

James tested the unlocked knob, stepped in, and stared.

Oh, this workshop was *sweet*. He didn't know a lot about them, but this looked comfortable to work in.

Peg boards hung along two walls. Several large shelves and chests of drawers housed more tools. Two tables were set up near the middle of the room, on either side of a table saw. Coolest of all, though, were the floor-to-ceiling windows along the back of the workshop. They looked out into Ryan's backyard and a patch of nature—trees and a stream below.

And they were on tracks. Two of them were open, ventilating the space to keep the burnt-wood smell down.

Ryan was working at one of the tables. He was shirtless, which was a *huge* distraction, but James managed not to stare at his sculpted chest and rippling abs. Instead, James glanced at his fingers—currently wrapped around a thin nail. He hammered it down in three blows. It looked like he was nailing in a backboard for some piece of small furniture.

"Hey," James greeted with a smile, his fingers closing harder around his backpack strap.

He'd worked hard to unlearn the kind of masculinity he'd always compared himself to. It was hard to remember that and not feel inadequate right now. Since he'd come out to his father, James had helped him with a few small home repairs, but nothing like this.

But he wasn't expected to *do* this, he reminded himself. He was just the accounting nerd, customer service face, and all-around details minder.

"Hi," Ryan answered as he hammered the last nail into place. He tossed the hammer onto the table and rolled out his shoulders as he came around the table to grab his shirt. "Sorry, I lost track of time."

"It's okay," James quickly answered, his eyes flickering once more down that hard body. Warmth tingled through him, his dick twitching slightly. The biological one, of course, not the silicone prosthetic that he relied on to pass the visual and grab tests. That one needed a rod to get hard. He was lucky that his boners were a lot less conspicuous unless he was naked.

Good thing, because sweat trickled down Ryan's muscled back when he turned his back to grab the shirt from a peg on the wall. James's gaze followed the droplet down to the small of his back and the low-slung jeans around his hips.

Christ, Ryan was hot.

James tore his gaze off his new business partner and almost threw his backpack onto the table. He winced at the clunking sound of the binder inside hitting the metal surface.

"I've got a binder."

Ryan looked confused, but he carefully nodded as he buttoned up his shirt and approached at an ambling pace. "I read about them."

It took James a second before he burst out laughing. Ryan thought he meant a chest binder. "No, a *binder*. Of papers."

The mortified expression that crossed Ryan's face made James laugh so hard he had to brace his hands on the table. "S-Sorry!" Ryan exclaimed. "That seemed weird, out of the blue, but—" Ryan started to stumble over his words, and James just held up his hand.

"S'fine," James grinned. Ryan had been researching trans stuff since their coffee meeting? That put him about a mile ahead of most people he came out to. "I don't have to wear *that* kind of binder anymore."

Ryan's cheeks were still red. He was trying to push past it, though, as he strode to the sink to rinse his hands off. "Oh! Congratulations."

"Thanks." God, Ryan was cute when he was flustered. "Hence my need for, you know, a job. And money." At the confused look, he added, "Had to do it on a credit card. It's not covered provincially."

"Ohhh. Right. So, how do we get started?" Ryan was ready to go, approaching the table and rubbing his hands together, all business.

James admired that go-get-it attitude. It energized him, too. "I did our market research on the other woodworkers in the area, what prices they charge, what they sell. In the process, talking to them, I found out that most people seem to specialize in one type of product, or at least one scale. The guys who do outdoor furniture mostly do *just* that. The kitschy gift stalls make all the wine bottle racks and front door signs."

Ryan was nodding. "I knew that."

"So, you build…" James squinted at the piece Ryan had been building when he came in. "What, primarily?"

Ryan grabbed it and hefted it upright. It was a shelf that stood about three feet tall. "A lot of practical stuff—shelves, trunks, furniture. I just got into small-scale work, though. I made that ring box I mentioned for my friend."

"Oooh, right," James grinned. That was sweet. Ryan came off as a closet romantic. "Can I see any examples?"

Ryan pushed away from the table to rummage around bins in one of the shelves. He came back with a handful of cubes made from different woods, which he scattered across the table. The designs instantly caught James's eye. All were in an unfinished state—some missing hinges or lids.

"Prototypes, obviously," Ryan explained.

"Right." James picked up one, running his thumb along the dark wood. This one was almost done, with hinges and a clasp. When he flipped it open, the inside was still rough. "This one's eye-catching."

"That was his second choice," Ryan said.

James nodded to himself. He rummaged through his binder to pull out a pricing spreadsheet. "Let's create a product line."

Ryan let out a sigh, and James looked up at him with a frown, but Ryan was grinning. "Oh, thank God. Just tell me what to make and I'll do it. I'll even make ring boxes."

"You like to be ordered around?" James teased, uncapping his pen with his mouth.

Ryan winked, and James tried to ignore the way his heart soared. They both knew this wasn't serious, but he'd forgotten what it was like to just idly flirt with a buddy.

That was all this was, after all.

CHAPTER

Seven

RYAN

James knew his shit.

It took a while for Ryan to list everything he'd built for friends and family over the last couple of years. He had to answer James's questions about material costs and how long it took him to build things. It was kind of sexy watching him punch numbers into his calculator, his brow furrowed like an accountant's.

He worked with numbers a lot himself, and James was able to do a surprising amount of mental math too. God, geeks were cute.

He pushed the thought away as James pushed a list across the table.

"Whoa."

It looked like a price list—wine racks for eighty bucks, shelves starting at a hundred, coffee tables for a couple hundred. Simpler items like small boxes started at twenty. The list just went on from there.

"Isn't this what everyone else makes?" Ryan asked. He might not go to craft fairs as such, but he did talk to other carpenters in town. He'd been down to the farmer's market, too. There were enough plans on Pinterest for wine racks that he knew he was going to have competition with this kind of product mix.

"Yes, which is exactly what we want," James told him, leaning over the table. They were sitting on bar stools on opposite sides of his work table, the paperwork spread out between them.

"But..."

"It's not competition. The reason people are selling them is because they already sell," James explained. Though he was trying to explain something he knew far better than Ryan, he wasn't condescending. "So you meet an existing demand instead of trying to create a new one."

That made so much sense Ryan didn't know what to say. "*Oh.*"

"The lightbulb moment, huh?" James laughed. "I've watched that look a lot. So many people figure they'll do something brand new and inventive. People don't want that. They want a wine rack for Uncle Greg, or... or a *home, sweet home* sign for Mom's front door."

"But we can put a new twist on some of these things, right?"

"Bingo," James nodded. "The same thing, but with fancy scrollwork or wood-burnt designs or something on the wine rack. Or a *Mr. and Mr.* sign for the front door..."

"I'll sell about six of those," Ryan laughed richly. "All to my friends."

"Hey, you might be surprised," James grinned. "Just having one or two pieces can get you custom work. But I won't let you stock an inventory that won't sell. At least, I'll try not to." His smile faded, and Ryan leaned in as he looked more serious. "This isn't a business I know *very* well. This is just my week's research."

"I know," Ryan assured him. James's concern was sweet, but he knew the risks of starting a new business. Yeah, it was possible he'd end up with bins of unpopular kitsch, but there was no other way to learn what was hot until he started to sell. He couldn't do that without inventory. "I've been saving to start this up. I can afford some losses." A starting salary for a carpenter at his company was high enough that he didn't worry about it.

"That's the other thing. I… I obviously can't contribute financially to the material costs yet—" James began. He fidgeted with his pen as he frowned his apology.

Ryan reached across the table to quiet him by putting a hand on his arm. "You're putting a shitload of time into this instead. I'll claim material costs from our profits first, but not labor. You tell me when you need money for startup costs—website locations or whatever you texted about last night—"

"Hosting," James laughed.

"That," Ryan waved a hand and laughed. "The profits, once we recover our out-of-pocket costs, are shared fifty-fifty. That's what the lawyer's drawing up already, isn't it?"

"It is," James confirmed, letting out a quick breath and smiling at him again.

"Perfect."

Ryan wasn't worried for a second. For him, it was more of a side business. It wasn't like he was planning to quit his job to sell tacky garden edging fences. James had more to lose, so even if he was putting less into it upfront, Ryan trusted him to make good on his word.

"Now, grants, and the business plan." Ryan groaned, and

James laughed. "I'm not letting you get away without reading what I have written to submit." James rubbed his hands together as if he were cold.

Ryan pulled the next folder toward him, then waved around the workshop. "This isn't exactly the most comfortable place to work from, is it? You can come into my house for coffee and warmth."

"Oh, if it's no trouble. If you feel more comfortable—" James started, and Ryan rolled his eyes.

"Get your ass inside before your fingers fall off," Ryan instructed him. "Besides, I can write off part of my house as an office that way."

James's answering laugh, warm and rich, made a pleased shiver run down Ryan's spine. Under any other circumstance, inviting him in for coffee could mean something else, but… it was too late for that.

Business and pleasure didn't mix.

Eight

CAM

"Earth to Mr. Carpenter, come in?"

Noah snapping his fingers in front of Ryan's face made Cam laugh. Polite as he was around strangers, his boyfriend was so cheeky to their friends.

Ryan laughed, too, as he shook his head. He'd been staring off across the barbecue while Jackson and Chase pretended to argue over who had to prep the salad for their Sunday get-together. "Sorry."

Alex, private investigator and always the perceptive one, was watching Ryan. "What's on your mind? Besides the new business?"

"Just that," Ryan admitted. "It's a big step."

"Of course!" Cam agreed. "And with a new business partner. I mean, Jay knows him, so I trust him, but…"

Ryan's response was quicker and more defensive than Cam expected. "He's solid." He didn't elaborate on *why* exactly he trusted the guy to build and market the whole business for him, except the allure of half the profits.

Cam swapped looks with Jackson, then Noah. Chase was

the one who said what everyone was thinking: "So, *how* cute is this guy?"

"Pretty cute, if I remember right," Noah chimed in, his eyes twinkling mischievously. He slid open the patio door and beckoned Jackson to check on the burgers for him. "And if I remember Ryan's double-take right."

Ryan's cheeks flushed, but he didn't have a chance to defend himself before Noah slid the glass door shut.

"I'm—I'm not—"

Noah pointed at the door, then his ear, and shrugged, his head tilted. *Can't hear you*, he mouthed.

Cam snorted with laughter, then punched Ryan's arm. "So, *is* he cute?"

"It's business now."

Aha. Ryan wasn't outright denying the possibility for attraction. Cam knew Ryan well enough by now to know what that signaled: he'd be interested if he felt he could be. He was old-fashioned that way. He'd never been on Grindr, and from their conversations about hookups, they were rare for him.

That thing with Isaac last year had been an exception, and look how that turned out. Cam's blood still boiled at the memory of catching Isaac at the grocery store a month after the breakup. Cam had chewed him out for lying about moving out of town after Ryan had talked about his feelings —a rare move for a guy like Ryan.

Since then, he must have *really* moved, because none of them had stumbled on him again, which was unusual for a town this size.

But since that breakup, Ryan had shown zero real interest in romance or being set up with anyone... until now.

"That's tough," Alex agreed. He leaned into Thomas on

the couch and absently rubbed the back of his boyfriend's neck as Thomas closed his eyes. "You've been looking livelier, though."

Cam nodded in agreement, along with several of the others as Jackson and Noah came back in bearing plates of hot barbecued food.

"Having something to do besides work for The Man is kinda nice," Ryan admitted. "Even if it's weird. Anyway, how was the week for you guys?"

"Busy," Cam told him. "Just pulled off the last of the honey, starting to feed the bees. I have to inspect the ones at home here—"

"You should wait until we've got everyone over," Noah interrupted. Cam raised his brows.

"Wait, why?"

"Not all of us have seen inside."

"Yeah," Jackson chimed in. "Floyd and Greyson wanted to see how it works too."

Cam thought that was weird, but he could see the point. "I don't have enough bee suits for everyone."

"That's fine, we'll stay back," Jackson nodded. "But before the bees go away for the winter—"

"They don't *migrate*," Cam rolled his eyes with exasperation.

"I meant hibernate, or whatever," Jackson defended with a laugh. "Before then, it'd be cool to show everyone."

That did actually sound kind of neat. Cam agreed with a shrug. "Cool. When's our next chance? Has to be a cloudy day, not too warm or cold. Actually, isn't everyone coming over next weekend for our end-of-summer thing?"

"Mmhmm," Noah nodded, looking pleased with himself. "And I checked the weather. It's good for beekeeping."

Noah had been around bees longer than Cam had, since it was *his* uncle Cam worked for and had learned from. Still, Cam felt proud when Noah showed off bits of knowledge.

Ryan was gazing off again, looking kind of distracted, and Cam nodded at him, then grinned at Noah. He leaned in to kiss him, ignoring his brothers' groans. "Sounds perfect. Just like you."

Noah beamed back at him, warm and solid tucked in against his side. He pecked his lips. Those bright eyes were fixed warmly on him.

"Oh, God." That was Ryan, in a mumble. He'd snapped back to. "Slap me if I ever do that."

Cam burst out laughing, his arm around Noah for a moment. He patted his boyfriend's ass and let him go to grab the condiments.

All things considered, Ryan had put up with being the only single guy in their crowd pretty well. Cam had a feeling that wasn't going to last for long. From the sly looks being exchanged between his brothers and their boyfriends, everyone was thinking the same.

CHAPTER
Nine

JAMES

"You're still paying off your card?"

James bit back an annoyed grind of his jaw as he looked over his dinner plate at his mother. Mom's tone made it clear that she still thought he'd been "impulsive and reckless" to put the surgery on his credit card.

"Yes."

She made a *hmm* sound and focused on eating again while he tensed up, waiting for the next verbal assault.

Try as he had, he'd never been able to make her understand how damn important it had been to him. First, it had helped him in being read as male full-time, instead of some weird, awkward combination of reactions from different people. Second, it had given him one fewer thing to direct his self-hatred at.

He generally loved himself these days, and it was an odd change. Freeing, to say the least. Sure, there were bad days, and he wasn't *thrilled* with his body, but who was? Now, he could actually nod and smile when people tried to relate to him by saying they had body features they didn't like. Before, he'd had to grit his teeth and try not to snap at them.

These days, he didn't look in the mirror and promptly want to go to bed again and never wake up. Until someone made him second-guess himself, or tried to force the issue with false concern—concern-trolling, it was called—or hatred. Someone like his mother.

But what if you're not sure? I'm just worried for you.

He'd once hoped that afterward she would see how much happier he was and understand. But no, she still didn't.

"I was thinking… James…"

He could hear the air-quotes around his name; she still spoke like she expected it to be a phase, some kid wanting to be called Batman.

"If the debt is burdening you, you know we can help."

It wasn't the offer it sounded like. James knew *that* by now. It would come with strings attached. *Forgive us the slips of name and pronouns,* or *laugh along when we joke about you.* Then, *take the jobs we tell you to take* and *move where we tell you to move, because now you owe us and we can hold that over you.*

To be fair, his stepfather wasn't as bad as his mother. Robbie was out of town for a couple months at a time, including right now. He didn't understand, but he'd started out a pretty decent guy. It was the fucking church she dragged him to. That, and an unwillingness to get between mother and son—or mother and daughter, as Mom still said —that kept him from saying anything.

"Thanks, but I'm good," he answered, as always.

She smiled and picked up her fork again. "However much you change," and he didn't miss that implication, "you're still my little girl."

She's talking loud enough for people to overhear. It was

unconscious by now: James swept the room with his peripheral vision. He checked for nearby waiters or tables, seeing who was around to hear it.

He'd started "living as male," however bullshit that phrase was, the moment he'd moved out to Fredericton. Most people, those he'd had to show ID to aside, knew him as a guy. Some people didn't even know he was trans. Not as many as he'd like, but some. And he tried to be careful about who found out. Random strangers knowing was a great way to get beaten up in a parking lot.

James's mom had no idea how much it took to hold his temper in check. He bit back the resentment and anger, a now-familiar taste in his mouth. Then, he licked the welt on the inside of his cheek. "Your son," he said tightly.

Mom glared at her salad. His mother's expression warned him not to talk about it, so he looked down at the table.

They pushed back their plates in silence, and his mother signaled the waiter for the bill. While they waited, she looked back at him. "I hope you put that degree of yours to use."

"Actually..." James began, then hesitated. *Wait. No. I don't want her finding out about this and meddling. She'll find out from a friend of a friend who goes to a market. But I can put that off.* "I have some ideas. Making contact with small business owners."

"You know Greg, who owns the gas bar?" Did he know Greg who owned the gas bar? The guy he worked for that summer at the car wash—when he'd been the oddball in a group of bikini-clad girls and shirtless guys hoping for tips? Duh. He hadn't been away *that* long. James resisted the urge to be sarcastic and just tightly nodded. "Well," his mother continued like she didn't notice his eye-roll, "he's hiring. If you grew out your hair..."

"Guys with long hair don't go over well back home, Mom," James reminded her. He had to steel himself for another skeptical eye-roll in response from her. Sure enough, there it was. "I'm fine, but thanks."

"If you insist," she responded. "I told him you might be looking for a job and he said he would have hired you back."

They didn't say much until they got out to the car, the tension almost at a breaking point.

It always seemed to be at that point: sizzling, red-hot, ready to explode if not for both of them holding back harsher words. Not that there was much point—they'd both said them before.

But that was what it was like on his mom's side of the family. Everyone smiled in public, however forced it was, and then had it out in private. Told each other they were going to regret it later—but so far, neither of them had been right.

At least he had an okay relationship with his dad. Talk about breaking the stereotypes.

"Will you be visiting soon?" his mother asked once she got to the car. "Do you need a ride anywhere before I go?" She was on her way to some important government meeting. As always, she'd stopped to see him and lecture him on his poor life choices beforehand.

"For Thanksgiving, at least, yeah. And no. I'm walking around for... job stuff," he told her, waving. "Gotta go."

She paused, tugging her skirt down and looking him over critically. He prepared for more critique: he hadn't shaven in a few days, and his stubble was thick and hard to ignore. One more reason it shocked him that she could even default to *my little girl* anymore.

Everything had changed, but she refused.

His mother was quiet for a moment, and James's heart rose. Sometimes, just occasionally, she seemed to take a step back and think about what she was saying. Now and then, he could pretend they had a good relationship.

"Take care," she told him, reaching out for a hug. "And call me if you need anything."

James couldn't say no to that—couldn't take the moment to call out that bullshit. He leaned in and squeezed her in a quick, manly hug, then kissed her cheek before he pulled back.

"You too. You look good, Mom. You'll rock the meeting."

Her face cracked in a quick smile. Normally, she might have enthused about where she got the skirt, how lovely he'd look in that shade of cream. For goddamn *once*, she didn't. She just waved off the compliment, thanked him, and said goodbye as he walked toward the hardware store downtown.

Sometimes it was the little things that meant the most.

"You met your mom today? Dude, I'm sorry." Jay winced as they rifled through the stack of checks. "Did it go better this time?"

James would never forget the spectacular falling-out he'd had here with his mom last Christmas, or the gesture of friendship when Jay had found him in the bathroom afterward to silently hug him.

"Yeah... I think so."

Since then, of the few friends he talked about family issues with, Jay was one.

"Good. Here's yours."

Plus, Jay had been cool with making out checks to his old

name before he could get it changed on his fucking bank account. That was something else he didn't like to think about, because it pissed him off.

James smiled every time he saw *James White* on a check now. Sure, his bank still called him Miss on the phone sometimes, because the shitty province wouldn't update his birth certificate. There was just no policy at all for that yet. But it was another small step.

"Thanks. She offered to help me with the surgery debt," James rolled his eyes.

Jay nodded, looking wary. "And? Just for no reason?"

"I know, right? She didn't say. The catches will be numerous, believe me."

"Right," they nodded. "Sorry."

"Oh, it's okay. It went better than it could have." James flicked the check against his fingers. "And there's better news. Your friend Ryan?"

It took Jay a second. "Oh, Noah's friend? The carpenter? Yeah?"

"I'm working with him on starting his new woodworking business. Fifty–fifty profit share, I do all the legwork, he does the manufacturing."

Jay's face split in a grin. "Dude! Good work!"

"Thanks," James grinned back. "He offered, just out of the blue. I guess I impressed him—"

"Oh, you did." Jay didn't often tease him, but the smirk on their face as they sipped their coffee was unmistakable.

James shot them a *really?* look.

"What? He was *so* checking you out," Jay laughed, shrugging widely. "I couldn't *help* but notice."

"We're going to be *running a new business together*," James emphasized, kicking Jay lightly. "You of all people know what that's like. I don't need any temptation."

"Mmmm. He *is* tempting," Jay smiled into their coffee cup, then almost choked with laughter when James blushed. "You thought so too. I saw you checking him out right back. I knew it!"

James rubbed at his face and pocketed his check, trying not to laugh. "You're a jerk. I have to go buy tools."

"Oooh—"

"*Jay*," James burst out laughing now, unable to help it. "Not *that* equipment. I'm pretty sure he's a top, anyway." The muscles on him? The way he walked with that rolling swagger?

"You can't just assume that," Jay winked.

"I know, I know."

God, James hadn't gotten laid in forever. He had to get out to their nightclub—the only one in town, or in the whole area—soon. Most of his Grindr messages lately were guys asking him what FTM meant and whether he was hung. He didn't have time for that.

"Anyway," Jay laughed, "I'll catch you around. Let me know how it goes."

"See you next week," James waved. Though he rolled his eyes on the way out the door, he was smiling, too.

So far, Ryan seemed sweet, trusting... perhaps *too* trusting... and well-grounded. And his sense of humor was awesome. James didn't mind teasing when it was coming from a guy as hot as him.

Fuck, now Jay has me thinking about him all over again.

Then again, what was the harm in daydreaming on his walk to the downtown hardware store?

CHAPTER
Ten

RYAN

"How's it going, Tan?" Unusually for him, Ryan didn't wait for an answer before he plunged ahead. "I can't do overtime starting next week. Just thought I'd give you a heads-up now."

Tan looked like he had to sit down—not with worry or outrage, but pure surprise. "You don't want overtime? Did you suddenly get a, uh, someone special?"

Ryan's lips twitched at Tan's inability to say the word *boyfriend*. To be fair, it could be out of consideration. Not everyone around the job site knew—tradesmen coming in for the day's work, for example. "Nah, not quite. Starting a business."

Ryan had talked to Tan about it before, so Tan lit up with a smile of recognition. "Selling things? You're finally doing that?"

"Why does everyone say *finally*?" Ryan grumbled.

Tan laughed. "Cause you've been making stuff for years, maybe?"

"Well..." That was true. Even back in high school after

woodworking class, Ryan had been making and selling simple stuff—birdhouses, mainly—to his mom's friends. He'd just never opened it to the public, per se.

It was lunchtime. Ryan shrugged off his jacket so he didn't get insulation bits in his food.

Tan nodded. "See? About time you got paid properly for it."

"Thanks." Ryan punched Tan's arm and took the sandwich he offered, strolling out with him to the front step of the half-finished house. He picked his way around a pile of boards and scraps of insulation.

They sat on the porch, legs dangling off the edge, coffee and sandwiches in hand. He didn't care if *some* people thought him eating lunch with the boss was sucking up. He and Tan had been buddies for longer than he'd worked for him.

They'd first met a couple of years before that, actually, at the town lumberyard. They'd been competing to buy the same load of discount lumber—each on their company's behalf. Ryan had been working as general help for another company while he learned the ropes, before his formal apprenticeship. Though Tan had won that battle, they'd wound up striking a friendship at a bar that night.

"What's up?" Ryan asked Tan, giving him another quick sideways glance. He seemed subdued today. Ryan wasn't sure Tan would want to talk about it, but he'd test the waters.

"Oh, you know. Stressed about deadlines."

That *did* make Ryan feel guilty. After all, he'd just ditched overtime shifts from now on. But God knew he'd been working them all summer.

Tan held up a hand before Ryan could think much more about that. "I'm not blaming you," he added firmly. "God, go start your business. I think that's great. Just… some people aren't pulling their weight."

Ryan knew exactly who Tan meant—Roger—but he didn't comment. He nodded.

"The boss is noticing, and I have to deal with it. I hate dealing with it. Why can't people just treat it like a real job, not make me have to babysit?"

Ryan winced in sympathy.

"Pretty much everyone here is great," Tan hastened to add, "but those one or two, oh boy."

Roger had to make up half of the problems on Tan's desk. Frankly, Ryan didn't know why he hadn't just let him go already. Except that would leave them shorthanded on guys who could do the precise work they needed on interiors. When he did show up, Roger did good work.

He just spent too much time across the border. He liked gambling and drinking at the backwoods strip bars in Maine, telling his wife it was trips with his buddies. Ryan knew the kind of places Roger went to. It wasn't his place to tell her what she already probably suspected, though.

"That aside… everyone else has been stepping up," Tan determinedly continued, as if not to end on a negative note. "We're just about winter-proof already. If we can get some extra families moved in before Christmas, that'd be great."

That was the secret target they all wanted to hit: getting more families their new homes in time for the holidays. Ryan felt another thrill of resolve with the reminder.

Sam came up to them with a grin and wave, clutching her travel mug of coffee. She'd been off for lunch for longer, so she'd probably headed home to check on her kid. Her boyfriend had been killed in a head-on collision with a moose three years ago.

His parents watched her five-year-old for now. She worked as much as she could now, knowing that when he was older, summers would be her busiest season and his free time from school. That wasn't going to be a nice schedule to figure out.

"What's happening?"

"Hey, Sam. Overtime's going," Ryan told her.

Sam's face lit up as she looked at Tan. "Really? I'd have to check with my mom, but…"

"Yeah, you get the next shot at it. I'll wait to hear back from you," Tan promised her with a smile.

"Thanks!" Sam sat on the edge of the porch and kicked Tan. "Dude, you should *see* what Ricky fucked up today."

Tan looked hesitant, the coffee cup raised halfway to his lips. "Do I want to know?"

"Yeah, he fixed it with a *really* clever dado," she laughed. "I'll show you when you're over there."

As Ryan settled into chatting with Sam and Tan, he dug out his phone to send a text to James.

How's it going? Just quit overtime shifts starting next week.

Moments later, he had his answer.

Awesome!! My lawyer friend has the letter of intent ready to go and I picked up the parts you asked for. I think.

Ryan chuckled.

Send a pic.

Moments later, he had it, and he zoomed in on his phone, bringing it close to his nose.

"Uh oh. Someone's getting dick pics," Sam commented as he checked out the hinge size and answered.

Yeah perfect! thanks.

It took him a moment to realize that comment had been aimed at *him*. It took him one more moment for his brain to realize he wouldn't mind that. Ryan's head snapped up as he stared at his friends. "Hey!"

Shit, he was blushing. Oh, they were *never* going to let this go, and Tan and Sam's laughs were both wicked.

He was screwed.

"Business shit. My new business partner picked up some hinges, that's all."

"For what?"

"Wedding ring boxes."

"Oooh, he moves fast," Sam smirked, leaning back against the porch post. She raised one knee to prop her coffee on it.

Ryan eyed her but decided to laugh anyway. Normally he'd have laughed at the idea of him getting married to *anyone*. But that was before he'd met someone who got his life into order without blinking twice, put up with his bad jokes and attempts at flirtation, and pushed him into doing what he'd always wanted to do, all at once.

When he thought about it, it actually terrified him that he didn't take it as a joke immediately.

You've known the guy all of a week and a half! Knock it the fuck off.

A moment later, his phone chirped with a text message, and Sam imitated the chirp.

He flipped her off and checked.

Free to meet tonight?

Ryan didn't have to bother checking his calendar.

Yep come on over. I've got freezer Chinese.

James's response was fast.

I'll bring the fortune cookies.

Ryan turned his phone more toward himself as he answered. He ignored the others in the background trying to sneak looks at his phone.

You're already bringing the luck. :)

James's response was a single smiley emoticon. He took that as permission to end the conversation and pocket his phone again.

When he saw the smirks on Tan's and Sam's faces, he rolled his eyes. "Oh, grow up."

Was he really that desperate for a hobby and a date? Everyone around him was so thrilled that he'd finally started a business, and was doing it with another guy who happened to be fucking adorable.

His friends laughed but let it go, talking sports instead until their lunch break was over.

CHAPTER
Eleven

JAMES

THIS TIME, INSTEAD OF HEADING TO THE WORKSHOP, JAMES knocked on the front door of Ryan's house. He shifted from foot to foot, trying not to feel like he was here for a date.

It didn't help when Ryan answered the door in a tight t-shirt that showed off *all those biceps*.

"Hey!" Ryan beamed and James dragged his eyes up to his face, grinning back at him. "Come in."

"Ohhh, God, that smells good," James groaned. It took him a second to realize how sexual his moan had been, and he laughed sheepishly. "Sorry. Hungry."

He wasn't eating well these days. He already had oatmeal most mornings, as much as he wanted to blow his food budget on Cap'n Crunch. For other meals, he ate a lot of rice and beans. At least being veggie was financially practical, as well as the right choice for him. He saved a lot of money on meat. The tricky part was fresh veggies, but he'd gotten pretty creative with frozen.

It was a terrible juggling act: trying to keep enough in his checking account to live while paying as much as he dared to the credit card company so the interest didn't fuck him over in the long run.

Needless to say, he hadn't had Chinese in a while.

"I've got the table set," Ryan jerked his thumb toward it. "You bring my hinges?"

"Don't worry, dude, I've got your hinges." James laughed and shrugged off his backpack, setting it by the door. "And I talked to someone about an ongoing contract—we'll chat after food."

He was proud of that one. He'd stopped by a custom jeweler—a little mom-and-pop operation—to ask whether any customers showed interest in local products.

The jeweler had loved the idea. Supporting local businesses was the trend of the day. Being able to put a locally-made ring in a locally-made box would thrill them. Not everyone would take the option, but some would. It could be occasional, but steady, work for them.

Ryan lit up. "Thanks! Sounds great. How was your day?"

Before he knew it, James was sitting at the table. Supper was veggie spring rolls, from-frozen orange tofu, and fried rice for him. Ryan chowed down on orange chicken.

He couldn't remember the last time a date had cooked a tofu version of a meal just for him, let alone a business partner.

But it was exactly what Ryan would do—had done—because Ryan seemed to respect him. He still felt a bit like an impostor, barging in and taking over this business to make it from scratch. Ryan's trust in him went a long way toward alleviating that.

It helped that when he started talking about parts prices for the boxes and sale prices, Ryan listened intently.

In fact, Ryan seemed to listen well in general. James

wasn't even self-conscious about how much he talked with Ryan listening.

Once supper was over, Ryan cleared up the dishes, then brought him to the living room while James explained the ring box contract.

"So, it's an occasional commitment?"

"Well, I suggested we sell them a small batch of premade examples with local designs—fiddleheads, lighthouses, things that he thinks are likely to be popular. We'll go from there."

"Great," Ryan agreed, nodding once. "I like the idea. Thanks for doing all that legwork on it."

James smiled. "It's my job," he reminded Ryan. "So you want me to say yes?"

"Yep."

"Our first real sale, then," James told Ryan, grinning at the looks of surprise, then pleasure, that crossed Ryan's face.

"I suppose it is. Cool."

Ryan seemed reserved in general, so getting that kind of smile from him made James happy, too. "So! Let's work out the letter of intent before we finish up, too."

"Oh! Right. I was ready to go on just a handshake," Ryan chuckled.

James glanced up at him, startled. "Really?"

"I know it's stupid," Ryan laughed. "But if I could, that's the way I'd do things. I get why we should do this, though, don't worry. Bring it on."

Ryan always seemed willing to get going as soon as James nudged him, and James appreciated that. "Right," he nodded, sliding a copy into Ryan's hand.

They settled back to read and discuss it. In particular, the profit share, joint bank account access, and decision-making power were important to go over.

In essence, Ryan was the head of manufacturing, while James was the head of marketing. All decisions were to be made jointly when possible. The letter probably wasn't finalized; they'd add to it as they realized what issues were likely to arise. For now, it was good enough.

That, plus a handshake after they signed.

Ryan's palm was huge around his, but gentle, his smile genuinely warm. James's worries slipped away, replaced by determination.

He wasn't going to screw this up. Ryan had faith in him. In return, even though Ryan was said he was worried about competing with existing woodworkers, James reassured him. Based on what he'd seen of Ryan's work already in the garage, he was confident.

Whatever happened, it was worth a shot, and he'd chosen a good business partner.

Now, if only he didn't feel sparks crawling up his spine when Ryan's hardened palm dragged across his own and they let go of their handshake.

CHAPTER
Twelve

RYAN

"It must suck not having a car." James made a face at him, those full lips drawing down into an expressive pout, and Ryan laughed. "Sorry."

"It *does* suck. So much. I can't wait until I get one," James chuckled. He looked out the window as they drove over the bridge toward the farmer's market.

Ryan had finished some small product every day that week since their letter of intent was signed. He was proud that they had a sample inventory now. That inventory was now in the backseat and trunk of his car, destined for the office of the market manager.

"Were you waiting for a job?"

"Yep. I was hoping to get one downtown so I can wait a year or so before I get one, but..." James blew out a sigh. "Transit is so shitty."

Ryan had never been on a bus here. He'd been lucky to get a car from his parents at sixteen, though he'd had to work part-time at a gas station to pay for all the associated costs. He'd seen the buses down by the mall, though. "I've heard," he sympathized.

"Going to university was the worst of it, though," James shrugged. "Now that I don't have to leave the house every day, it's not so bad. It's going to be annoying as the business grows, though."

That did bother Ryan. If he weren't certain James would turn it down, and if they had steady sales, he'd sneakily set him up with a business vehicle. For now, that was a no-go. "We'll work around it," he promised. "Now that I'm not doing overtime, I can drive us to more meetings, and I can actually be there on our behalf. Rather than making you run around doing it all," he chuckled.

"Right," James nodded, his brows drawing together.

Ryan wondered what was on his mind, but he wasn't sure he should ask. "If you're okay with that," he added after a minute, turning onto the side road.

"No, I'm fine." James cleared his throat and nodded. "The manager's office is just around the side."

"Great." Ryan pulled up in the emptier section of the parking lot and climbed out. James headed to the back and waited for Ryan to unlock it. Then he gathered the smaller items—a mug stand, a carved box, and a cute *crazy cat lady* kitchen sign—into his arms.

James had persuaded Ryan to go with something safer than the signs they both wished they could sell. Straight people around here were their main market, so the *Mr. and Mr.* signs had to wait.

Ryan took the shelf under one arm and shoe rack under the other.

The manager had wanted to see samples of his work, so they were going to flood him with great-looking pieces.

Though he was clearly trying not to show it to Ryan, not

wanting to psych him out, James was nervous as hell. He kept licking his lips and taking deep breaths.

James had coached Ryan several times on their elevator pitch. He was going to do just fine, but Ryan still didn't blame him for being unnerved. This was a big opportunity to launch the business.

James balanced the box under his arm for a moment to ring the bell, then shifted the load around again.

The door opened a second later and the market manager—a tall guy named Angus—answered.

"Oh, hello again! James, wasn't it?"

James had been here last weekend to check into the market, so it was a good sign that he remembered him. At least, Ryan hoped it was a good sign.

"Yes, that's me! Hi. Angus, this is Ryan, my business partner and the mastermind behind the work."

"Great to meet you, Ryan. Let me give you a hand there."

Together, they carried the pieces over to the desk. Ryan did an inward jump for joy when he saw that he was already turning over the shoe rack in his hands with a skilled appraising eye. "Wow, the work on this is gorgeous."

Ryan grinned. "Thanks," he answered, setting down the other shelf and sitting in one of chairs he gestured them toward.

James sat next to him and scooted closer, his hands folded in his lap.

"I'm glad you came in to see me," Angus told them, leaning forward. "First, can I have a look at everything?"

"Go right ahead," James told him with a smile. "That's what we brought it for."

Angus looked at Ryan, who nodded his confirmation. He

picked up the pieces and started examining them. Ryan's foot tapped nervously, but he didn't plan to say much.

"What kind of wood is this?" Angus asked Ryan.

"This one's cedar," James answered. He'd memorized the list of woods in these pieces the first time Ryan had explained them to him—which was impressive for a non-trade.

"Oh, cool." Angus was still watching Ryan for a second, and then he switched to the mug rack. "Where do your designs come from?"

"Mostly his own plans," James supplied again, leaning forward to explain. "Some we buy and modify, but he's got a lot of clever ideas."

"Yeah, I like what you did with this," Angus agreed, pointing to the curly fiddlehead tips on the mug rack rods. "Very local." He grinned at Ryan.

"Thanks," Ryan nodded.

Once Angus was done examining the sign, he glanced up at them. "Why pick these things to show me? Is this your typical product mix?"

"We're just getting started," James explained, "as you know, but yes. We chose them all carefully, to sell. Customers look for these kinds of products as Christmas gifts." James had explained this to Ryan—they had to sell the idea that they'd make the customers happier than the other guy. The market manager was most concerned with keeping customers happy. They didn't know who the other guy was or what he sold, or if there even *was* another guy competing for the stall. If there was, they had to make customers happier than he would.

"Good thinking." Angus looked down at the box, then up

at Ryan again. "And this box is gorgeous. How long have you been creating woodwork crafts?"

James didn't answer this time, even though Ryan had told him when they developed the sales pitch—since high school. After a second, Ryan was the one to answer. "Since high school. I started off doing small pieces in woodworking class and then just... never stopped. I'm always tinkering. That started off as a ring box design, but my friend turned it down, so I turned it into something bigger. More practical."

"Great idea," Angus agreed. "People have a fascination with boxes."

"I think we're all secretly cats," James agreed, and that at least made Angus chuckle.

"So," Angus said, looking back at Ryan with a slight frown. "So, I love your work, but I have some mixed news."

Oh, boy. I bet they don't have any free space. Ryan nodded and waited, trying not to hold his breath. He could feel James's disappointment from beside him.

"When are you available to take a stall here?"

"We were hoping for one as soon as possible," James spoke up.

"Right." Angus looked at Ryan again.

It was then that Ryan realized this whole conversation had been Angus talking to him, not James, even though James was the business operations manager. Angus was friendly with him, even slapping his knee as he joked, smiling at him more as they chatted.

Oh, shit. The moment in the car had been real. *This is why James doesn't want me coming along to all the meetings.*

Ryan had always been the biggest in his class. He'd never had the problem of not being respected because he looked young and cute. At least, Ryan hoped that was what going on.

Hopefully it wasn't something transphobic or homophobic. He didn't get that feeling from the guy.

It was just the kind of man-to-man chat that James had probably always been excluded from.

"The thing is, we have another woodworker who approached us this morning. We're about to sign him on. That's our capacity," Angus told Ryan. "Can you join a waiting list?"

Ryan's gut clenched and he looked at James. "That's for my boss to tell me."

The hint was strongly worded enough that Angus glanced at James, back to Ryan, and then—at last—back at James. "Right. Do you think you can wait? We may get you in before Christmas when the market expands for the pre-Christmas weeks. It's just not right away."

James shot him a quick, grateful look, before he answered. "We can wait. If we get a spot at another market, though, we'll have to chat."

"No, go right ahead, look for opportunities," Angus quickly agreed with James. "No hard feelings. I hope we can get you in, for what it's worth. I like your attitudes and your work."

Whoever had scuppered them, Ryan wasn't resentful. It was just a disappointing setback. There were people who started businesses all the time, and it was sheer bad luck for them he'd gotten there earlier in the day.

James's jaw was tight with disappointment, though. They made conversation, gathered up their inventory, and escaped the office.

Ryan waited until they were over the bridge again before speaking up. "Do you get that a lot?"

"Get wha—oh." James grimaced. "Yeah, a fair bit."

"Just because you look young and cute?"

James laughed quietly and gave him a grateful glance. "Well, I guess there's the upside."

Ryan grinned. "I never get *cute*."

"Oh, no. You'll have to live with *perfect masc*, then," James rolled his eyes.

Ryan snickered with laughter. "That sounds like a Grindr buzzphrase to me. I've been told that's a thing there. I have never had someone call me a perfect masc in real life, where it counts."

"I'm admitting nothing," James retorted, but he was grinning.

"I think you already did," Ryan teased. He chuckled when he saw James's cheeks go red. "You got any hot dates?"

"Maybe I do," James defended himself with a pout. "It's the new age, dude. We're allowed to date online."

Ryan laughed. "Good for you. If I were more motivated, I'd do the same." It sounded a bit weird to meet people on apps, but more power to James for it.

He noticed the flicker of jealousy that went through him at the possibility of James having a date with someone else.

What if, when he fidgeted with his phone, he was finding dates?

God, he *was* jealous. He should get on that. Find himself a date, too. Before he started getting snarky with all his paired-up buddies.

James's house was one of those places that had been converted into apartments. When he dropped James off, Ryan realized he'd been smiling all morning. Even this much socialization was good for him. Maybe James had the right idea.

He waited until he got into his driveway before he sent the text.

Wanna help me get set up on that site sometime?

A minute later, he had his response from James.

Of course! we'll get your lame ass on dates too ;)

Ryan laughed and pocketed his phone, unlocking his front door. He was glad that James was comfortable enough to banter back now.

CHAPTER

Thirteen

JAMES

JAMES COULDN'T PRETEND, EVEN TO HIMSELF, THAT HE WASN'T jealous.

Would he help his friend set up a Grindr profile? Ryan wasn't great with technology. He probably didn't even have location services enabled. Of course he'd help. But he didn't have to like it.

He slammed the fridge closed for the fourth time in the last hour.

James wasn't heading over just to talk about Grindr profiles with Ryan. Too long a walk for that. He'd just heard back from both craft fairs coming up soon. One next weekend had a last-minute stall available, and the other had one a week later.

It was time to get serious.

It had been a few days since their unsuccessful farmer's market meeting. These last couple of weeks had been dawn-'till-dusk work days—the kind he hadn't realized he missed so much. The shitty work environment at the store had overshadowed the perks. James genuinely enjoyed talking to people and getting out of the house.

Again, James looked around his fridge for something to satisfy him before he walked over to Ryan's house. He wasn't sure what exactly he felt like eating.

Somewhere in the back of his mind, he remembered a lecture he'd once attended at school. The lecturer, a fourth-year student, had talked to the incoming class about staying healthy.

"The human body has primal needs—food, water, the bathroom, sleep, and yeah, sex. But the body doesn't always know which is which. Sometimes you feel hungry but you have water and you realize you were just thirsty? It's that principle. If nothing's hitting the spot, take a step back and check everything else."

It had proven true more times than he could count. Even when the depression was so thick he could barely see out of it, sometimes there was an extra layer of grey he didn't realize until it was gone. Usually after he'd eaten, or had a glass of water, or some stupid little thing like that.

James had the sneaking suspicion he knew which of those list was bothering him lately.

He had to get going, though, if he was going to have time to see Ryan before rock climbing tonight. He climbed at an indoor gym that was part of his old university.

Even though he'd graduated, community members could register for memberships and climb there anytime. Without a regular partner, he was limited to climbing when the group did, every week. Sometimes friends joined him, but nobody loved it as much as him.

"You do what?"

James laughed at the look Ryan gave his arms. "Yeah, I can climb walls. I'm stronger than I look," he complained. He elbowed Ryan as they walked between his house and his workshop.

"I'm sure! I wondered how you got so toned," Ryan grinned.

James yanked his attention quickly off the comment. Ryan noticing his slowly-honed core strength didn't mean Ryan *wanted* him. God knew he knew that much by now. "It's amazing what it does for you. You find muscles you didn't know existed."

Ryan laughed. "It's kind of equal-opportunity, isn't it? The bigger and heavier you are, the harder it is for you..."

"Exactly," James nodded. "It's bodyweight training, but on a vertical surface."

Ryan looked thoughtful. "Genius. Is there any kind of open night?"

"Every week! You wanna come tonight?" James followed Ryan into his workshop, flipping his binder open to the inventory page. "To the gym?" he quickly added... just in case.

He was definitely imagining Ryan's blush in the weird, sterile workshop overhead light. Ryan nodded. "I'd love to. Okay, here's what I've been working on..."

They had an easy, comfortable rhythm now as friends and business partners. They always whipped through the list of to-dos, should-dos, and have-dones in no time. Now, they had a target to work toward—the craft show next weekend. They were both laser-focused.

"Oh," Ryan spoke up, glancing at him. "I found out who

the other woodworking business was. My least—my coworker."

Had quiet, steadfast Ryan been about to admit that he didn't like someone? James's lips twitched, but he didn't call him out on it. "Oh, really?"

"Yeah. He didn't even tell me himself—Tan, my boss, told me."

James hummed under his breath. He couldn't comment much, but he frowned. "That sounds shitty."

"Yeah, whatever," Ryan shrugged it off. "Being free of that means we can do these craft fair things. Speaking of which, you wanted to show me the setup?"

"Oh! Yes. Our table's a six-foot one, do you have anything like that for us to set up?"

James didn't have all the decorations yet, but he explained what he was thinking: using larger items to elevate smaller items and create a visually interesting display; an email list signup form; and a credit card processing sign near the front of the table.

James could almost see Ryan's eyes glazing over, however the carpenter tried to hide it. He bit back his laugh.

"If you're fine with all that, I'll go ahead and buy it and we'll do a trial setup tomorrow night, here. If you're free."

"Of course I'm free," Ryan snorted. "I'm not the top Grindr pick of the week."

"There's not even—there's not a leaderboard," James retorted, but he laughed. It wasn't *that* unusual for guys not to have used it, but most at least knew how it worked. "Oh, Scruff has one…"

"I don't even know what that is," Ryan admitted, looking embarrassed as he laughed. "God, I'm lame."

"No," James assured him and clapped his shoulder. The thick muscles under his hand were warm and firm, and… he didn't want to let go, so he didn't just yet. "You just have self-respect."

Behind Ryan's sweet brown eyes, concern rippled as his brows pinched. He didn't say anything, which was typical for him, but…

"It's a joke," James grinned.

Then, Ryan relaxed enough to chuckle. "Okay."

James appreciated that Ryan was worried enough about him to notice that comment instead of just laughing it off immediately, though. How sweet.

"But if there *were* a leaderboard, would you be on the top?" Ryan grinned. That mischievous look was back in his eye.

James broke out laughing, staring at his new friend and letting go of his arm to fold his own arms, tilting his head. He didn't care how camp he looked doing it. "Are you asking if I get around?"

"No!" Ryan looked mortified now, his eyes widening as he raised his palms. "I meant, I bet you're popular, because you're cute. If you don't mind my saying so. And I wouldn't judge—"

James laughed even harder now. Ryan teased him so easily, but he took him seriously in return. *"Joking,"* he reminded Ryan, elbowing him before he clapped his back. "Come on, we should go climbing before you lose your shit." He didn't want to answer that question, but not because he was shy. It could just be a downer to get into the finer details of his interactions on that damn app.

Ryan thought he was *cute*. James didn't hate the word, but

he didn't prefer it. But Ryan could get away with calling him that.

It looked like Ryan was relieved to get the chance to escape. He strode for the workshop door, but held it for James behind him.

"Don't bother. You'll have a bulge no matter what you do."

Ryan's cheeks heated up as James murmured to him behind his shoulder. He'd been standing behind him and no doubt noticing the way he tugged his climbing harness this way and that.

"I wasn't—"

"Mmm." For his part, James didn't seem shy. The straps circled his crotch, showing the distinctive bulging outline in his pants.

Noticing that made it hard for Ryan to focus. He tightened the straps around his own legs, double-checking all the buckles and straps. The whole time, he tried to ignore his own package and the way James was restraining his laughter.

"I see why you like this sport," Ryan grumbled teasingly.

James wasn't perving on anyone else, though. He had ignored the other young, cute guys here since they'd arrived. After taking Ryan to the counter to get shoes and a harness, he'd shown him how to assemble the harness.

"Now check these." James hooked his thumb in the straps around Ryan's legs, pulling him closer.

Oh, shit, that was hot.

Ryan caught his breath. James's strength alone wasn't enough to budge him, but he was almost surprised enough to stumble. Which brought him to his other concern: the nimble fingers tugging at the straps around his crotch. He had nowhere to hide any possible… reactions.

"Um, so, we hold each other down? Or… up?" Ryan blushed at his own ignorance; he'd never thought twice about rock-climbing. It hadn't been a sporting option while growing up, and nobody else he knew did it.

Sure, Cam had once played hockey, and he'd mentioned wall-climbing now and then in cross-training. Chase fenced and dared anyone to tell him that wasn't a sport. Thomas and Alex skied together. Floyd and Greyson ran and worked out in the gym. Kevin and Matty were pro hockey players. That left Ryan and Jackson as just about the only two who didn't play sports, and even Jackson could be persuaded to join a pickup ball game in the summer.

It wasn't because Ryan was afraid of physical activity. He'd played football and soccer growing up, but never seriously. Nothing else had caught his attention. He didn't have the same competitive drive as many of his friends.

"Something like that," James grinned. "It's a counterbalance system."

That instantly made sense to Ryan. They used similar to lift loads of lumber by hand to upper stories sometimes, while framing a house. Machines were preferred these days. He was used to working in a harness when safety regulations called for it, too.

But here, it was different. There were no neat ladders to climb up.

Ryan stared doubtfully up the wall of flimsy-looking rubber handholds. He didn't see anyone else who looked a similar size and weight to him around right now.

"You'll be fine," James reassured him, and then a shiver ran down Ryan's spine. James's hand was resting on his back, his thumb rubbing a slow circle or two between his shoulder blades.

Ryan cast him an appreciative look, licking his lips subconsciously.

"But I can belay you—"

"What now?" Ryan knew exactly what James meant, but he wanted to see if he'd blush.

It was so easy to make James turn red. There he went again, those bright eyes lighting up in embarrassment. "You... I can't take you anywhere."

"Nope," Ryan agreed, then fell quiet to let James talk.

"I can belay you. The rope system makes it work."

"Yeah, I get it now. I've done it with supplies at work, just not... other guys," Ryan chuckled. He rolled his shoulders to limber up. "Am I climbing or belaying first?"

"I'll get you to climb first so you know what that side's like. I think it's better to climb, then belay," James told him matter-of-factly. He sounded like he'd taught this before.

Just another bit of expertise that made Ryan find him fascinating.

"Yes, sir," Ryan teased. "You're the boss."

"You don't seem to mind." Was that James flirting? The way he sauntered alongside of Ryan, leading him to the wall, made Ryan think so.

Ryan smirked. "As long as you do a good job of it."

"You'll see. Step forward."

Ryan obeyed, and James clipped and tied him in, showing him how the system worked. It was exactly what he'd expected, down to the figure-eight knot. There was a clever grigri with assisted braking in case of sudden falls.

"I actually hate these," James confided under his breath. "But they're safer for beginners, because it's harder to fuck them up."

Ryan's nerves were kicking in now. An unconscious shiver coursed through him when he looked at the wall. It stretched above him a good two stories or so, almost all the way up to the ceiling.

He'd been up on support beams and scrabbled across roofs, but that was a known environment. It was easier to get up and down. Here, he'd have to scrabble his way up, fighting for toeholds and handholds every step of the way.

"A little adrenaline's good," James told him. Ryan cast him another grateful look. "Keeps you on your toes. This one's an easy route though. Take it slow, think about what you want to do before you do it. You're not gonna fall far. I'll keep the tension tight to make sure of that."

Ryan blew out a breath and nodded firmly. He wanted to impress James... and he didn't want to think about why that was.

He stepped toward the wall as James stepped back, reaching up for the highest handhold he could grab. His foot naturally found a rubber spot. He dug his toes in, ignoring the pinch from the special shoes that pressed them together. After he grabbed the second handhold, he tensed his body and pushed up. His foot found a hold as high as he could make it go, leaving him crouched against the wall.

Almost instantly, the rope was tight—if he'd let go, he would have been swinging a couple of inches off the ground.

Some of the adrenaline faded as he took a look up, focusing only on the next couple of grips.

Once he was in motion, it was way easier to keep going than stop and think about it. He tried to keep moving steadily, letting no more than a few seconds pass each time before choosing the next handhold or toehold.

Everything else faded: the noise of the gym around them, the faint music in the background, the calls of belayers to their climbers from nearby...

James's voice and the wall were all that was left. He saw Ryan looking for that next handhold—the one that looked just a *bit* too far away, but maybe he could manage it...

"You going for it? Tension?" His warm, rough voice filtered up through the fog of unimportant information. Ryan nodded broadly so the motion could be seen from below.

"Tension," Ryan confirmed, raising his voice.

The rope tightened, and he tensed his whole body before launching up for the next handhold.

He made it, the adrenaline flooding to the very tips of his fingers and toes. He flattened against the wall. The grip was barely strong enough to keep him up there, but he had it.

He heard a cheer, and that was unmistakably James's. And a couple of other voices, too.

Oh, shit, other people were watching.

He brushed that off and ignored them, waiting a second before he chose his next awkward toehold. He was scrabbling up the wall, more like a crab than the graceful climbers he spotted in his peripheral vision.

It occurred to Ryan when he looked up and saw about six

feet to go that James had his life in his hands, and he didn't mind. James was cautious and methodical, thorough in everything he did. Why wouldn't he be thorough with Ryan's safety?

Ryan could feel how closely James was watching him—how quickly he responded whenever he called down for more or less tension.

Just a few feet to go. So close he could *almost* reach out and grab it. Jesus, that meant he was…

He looked down.

Though he was used to working on roofs, it was different to look straight down and see only the even-smaller figure of James. The rope was threaded along his front and above him, then down behind him, so he didn't even see the rope.

"Deep breaths," he heard James call out.

Ryan jerked his head in a quick nod, the adrenaline seizing up his muscles for a second. A few deep breaths, in and out for the count of four, helped release them. Then, he forced his gaze up instead, to the last few handholds.

The orange one. He could make that one.

Some fear-based response snaked through his nerves at the idea, but he pushed past it and lunged for it.

He missed, his fingers scraping the wall as his feet were jolted loose.

"Damn it. Grab on. Try again!"

He wasn't giving up now. James was right. James's coaching had gotten him this far, and it wouldn't fail him now.

Ryan found his toe holds again, then his hand holds, and made another lunge. He made it this time, every muscle in his back clenching to haul himself up until his feet could find a perch.

From there, it was easy to wrap his fingers around the top edge of the wall. Tension and anticipation flooded out of his body, replaced with triumphant joy.

Holy shit. He'd just climbed a wall with nothing more than his fingers and toes. It was the kind of accomplishment that felt strange even as he reveled in it—totally nerdy, and totally cool.

James's whoop of joy was unmistakable, and it made him break out laughing.

There were a few other cheers and claps from nearby; James's friends had been watching his last few moves, too.

"Let go!" someone called out. The face Ryan made must have been easy to see even from down there, because there was answering laughter. "No, seriously."

Ryan looked down at James, glad his adrenaline didn't spike this time, and James nodded. The rope was tight and secure in James's hands.

Okay, then.

Ryan slowly let go of his hand holds, then his foot holds, however wrong it felt to do so.

"Lean back. Like you're sitting on the sofa."

That was an even weirder instruction. But when James told him to do something and he was dangling thirty feet off the ground, Ryan did it.

It was almost like flying, if not for the strain against his legs and thighs from the straps of his harness. He caught his breath when the rope jolted, then started to shudder. The wall rose beside him.

Twice more, James had to remind him to sit back. He kept wanting to grab the wall to keep himself from hitting it, even though he knew the proper procedure. It was an instinct strong enough that fighting it took almost all his attention. The ground startled him with how close it was when he next looked.

A couple more feet and Ryan's feet were touching the ground, the rope going slack. He found his footing again and almost stumbled immediately.

James yanked a few more feet of slack free from the harness so he could haul Ryan in for a tight hug.

Oh, boy—especially after his adrenaline rush, the warm, smaller body tucked against his felt good. Arms snaked around his waist as James praised him.

He squeezed James in his own hug, a laugh slipping free. "That was fun."

James broke out laughing, along with a few others nearby.

Right. Shit. We're in public.

For a second, consumed by James and his help achieving this cool feat, Ryan had almost forgotten. He'd almost wanted to sweep him off his feet.

Ryan's cheeks heated up as he stepped back from James, suddenly aware of the bulge pressed into his leg. James's cock, framed by straps the same way his own was.

Had he felt that, too? Was it…?

Oh, shit, no, he scolded himself. The only reason he'd need to know whether that was stiffened skin or silicone was if he was interested.

And he wasn't. Well, more precisely, couldn't be. No, not even that. *Shouldn't* be.

In his moment of flustered embarrassment, trying to think his way out of that, he almost missed James's hands. He only felt them when they were on his crotch, unfastening the figure-eight knot.

Looking down his body at James's hands working around

his crotch did *not* help his current train of thought. He couldn't indulge it for any longer if he wanted to not embarrass them both in public.

"I got it," he told James. He was strangely disappointed when James listened, and his hands went to his own harness instead to slip the rope free.

Then, the positions were reversed—but James waited to get hooked in himself until Ryan was set up.

"Right. I'm gonna have a friend here to watch you belay me, but the basics are simple. I like a tight belay, so don't worry about that."

That's awfully distracting, too. Nope, don't.

Ryan paid the closest attention he could as he learned the familiar safety principles: always have at least one hand on the rope; never point his thumb that way; when taking up the slack, always have both hands on the rope; keep it angled down as much as possible.

It was different when it was James's weight on the line than a load of gear.

"Ready?" James asked him.

James's friend, Ash, was at their elbow, studying his technique. James hung onto the wall, about to take his first step.

"Ready."

It was instinctual to want to take up the slack the moment he felt any. He worked quickly to haul the rope through the harness, his eyes settling on James's lithe body splayed out across the wall.

Oh, that was hot.

Ryan was a good multitasker. He kept the part of his brain that was focused on the sexual appeal of a man in tight clothes and an even tighter harness stretched out on the wall in front of him separate from the part that wanted to keep him safe.

Most distractingly of all, the leg straps pulled the fabric of James's trousers tight around his thighs. Ryan had a great view of his ass.

He understood why James had been smirking when he hit the ground.

Ryan tried not to stare at it, but he had no choice if he wanted to anticipate his moves. It was easy to follow James's progress as long as he paid close attention. He must have been enough of a natural at belaying that Ash, near him, didn't offer many instructions.

Really, as long as he remembered to keep the rope down, it was easy.

"Oof—fuck," James hissed from about ten feet up. He'd lunged for a handhold, missed, and banged his knee against a foothold.

Ryan winced in sympathy and watched closely. He saw the next most obvious move a second before James did. He was ready by the time James scrambled to put his foot on the spot where he'd just bashed his knee. Then, James lunged again.

He took the slack in fast, barely feeling James's weight on the line. It made it almost tricky to belay him, because he didn't have much to tug against.

"Th-Thanks," James panted, grinning over his shoulder after he took a moment to catch his breath. "Nice. You're sharp."

The praise made Ryan grin back at him. "Welcome. Just about ready?"

"Just about."

Ash had started smirking into his Gatorade bottle as he

looked back and forth between Ryan's hands and James's position. Not in a mean way, but in the kind of way that definitely meant he was making the wrong assumptions.

He couldn't stop looking at James's sexy little ass, since he had no other view at all by this point. Ash could deal with a little sexual tension.

James made it to the top in half the time Ryan had. Then, Ash stepped closer to explain the *other* end of what he'd just experienced. "When he leans back, it protects his head from banging the wall if the rope slips. So you lift the rope like that—yes, exactly. And gently guide it through. Keep a hold on that, be ready to yank it down if it slips... exactly."

His hands were toughened from his line of work. He barely felt the rope burn as the cord slid through his palms and James lowered in front of him.

When James hit the ground, he sprang up to his feet and beamed. "Nice! Thanks, Ash."

"Hey, I think *I'm* supposed to congratulate *you!*" Ryan laughed, hauling more slack free. "Thanks," he added to James's friend as he walked off—clearly to give them a moment.

This time, when James leaned in, the hug wasn't impulsive and joyful. It was slow and deliberate and...

Hot.

Ryan swallowed hard, letting go of James after a second or two and stepping back. The part of him that wanted to pull James in and run his hands down his back to that tight little ass and kiss him...

"Phew. You want to climb again?" Ryan asked.

"Nah, I'm not feeling like it tonight," James told him, his voice low. "And you just learned a lot. Do you?"

"No, once was enough for me," Ryan admitted with a laugh. "I can give you a ride home."

James smiled. "Thanks. I'd appreciate it."

"Of course."

They were quiet as they climbed out of their gear and shoes, back into their normal clothes. Ryan tried not to notice his disappointment when the toned arms and the slender, muscled physique of his partner disappeared again under his sweater.

He was shivering.

After James said his goodbyes and Ryan politely nodded at everyone, they headed out to the car and Ryan glanced at him. "Cold?"

"A little," James admitted, his cheeks reddened by the cold. "They try to heat that place, but it doesn't always work. Especially in the winter."

It had felt warm enough to Ryan. He chuckled. "You do have poor circulation."

"Rude," James clicked his tongue with a waggle of his head, which made Ryan laugh. "Yeah, I do, though. You should have seen me pre-T."

Ryan grinned. "Yeah? It got better?"

"Dude, I was always in three layers before that. Now I can manage in two," James rolled his eyes, and Ryan laughed again. "You don't know how lucky you have it, you guys who are space heaters."

"You just need to find a big spoon."

Ryan's cheeks flushed the moment he said it. Would James take it as an invitation? Fuck, had he *meant* it as one? He was awfully tempted by the idea of wrapping his body around James's, pulling him in against his front. That would leave his hands free for an awful lot of exploration.

Shit, that was totally inappropriate.

James snickered. "I will. If you need a moment there, just tell me."

Ryan's body was flushed with heat, and oh yeah, that was a semi Ryan was trying to will away. Ryan shoved James, but James just snickered, his eyes bright with mischief. Ryan knew now what James felt like when he teased him.

"You're... Jesus, anyone ever tell you you're a handful?" Ryan retorted, adjusting himself. That would settle down. It was just adrenaline, plus innuendo and imagination. "Sorry," he added in the obligatory mumble as he headed around to the driver's side.

James's eyes glinted. "Oh, plenty of guys get them at the gym. No big."

By the time they climbed into the car, Ryan was ready to pretend that moment hadn't happened. James was being gracious enough to give him the chance to forget.

There *was* something still bugging him, though, but he wasn't going to ask.

"I don't have that problem, but I've got a few others," James added, buckling up. Those bright eyes were fixed on him, that cute smile playing at his lips as his face tilted up toward Ryan's.

Oh, shit, he's not gonna give me any space here. Ryan's hand nearly found James's instead of the parking brake. He caught himself just in time and squeezed the button extra-hard. *Keep it together.*

"Yeah?" Ryan asked casually, letting him say what he wanted to say.

James chuckled. "I saw you looking. It's not biological yet. Or maybe ever—I don't like all the options we've got, and there's not many options yet."

"Ahh. So you don't feel…?"

"Nope. Well, a bit of a phantom feeling, if you know what I mean," James told him. Ryan once again admired his simple openness. How many times had he answered these questions with the same good humor?

Or was he answering them because it was Ryan asking?

That was presuming way too much about what James wanted, surely? When James's eyes fell to his lips for a second, Ryan suspected maybe he was right, though.

"Ohhh. Yeah, I can imagine."

James nodded. "I don't always wear it. It helps in the bathroom. And when I top for the right guy, obviously… A lot of us will say *assembly required*, like IKEA."

Ryan was blushing, but he nodded, determined to let James talk. He clearly was comfortable with him as a friend, at least, and Ryan had to make it not-weird, right?

God, Ryan wasn't hard right now, but it had only barely faded. He could get… *inspired*… a little too fast. He wanted to roll down the window for cool air, but James would get cold.

"Right. So it gets… hard…?" Ryan trailed off.

"With a rod," James's eyes twinkled. "Which I did *not* put in, because otherwise it'll look like a boner with a harness on. And I don't know if we're at that stage of friendship yet."

He *was* flirting. A breathy laugh escaped Ryan as he grinned at James, pulling to a stop at the light. He had the chance to look over for a second at the high cheekbones and long lashes. A wicked smirk played on James's lips…

James knew exactly what he was doing.

Okay. Fine. Two could play the *flirting friends* game. Ryan's tongue flickered along his lower lip as he watched James. He said, "You're lucky. You get to choose your boners."

"Oh, not always," James grinned. "It's just not as obvious."

That got Ryan's imagination working again as he nodded at James.

Shit. I'm really into this guy.

Ryan missed the light turning green for the first few seconds. When James laughed and pointed ahead, he let go of the brake to start driving again. He'd only been there now and then to go over numbers in the last couple of weeks—James usually came to his place. "Just down this way, right?"

"Yep," James cheerily answered. "You're polite about it, you know."

Ryan wasn't sure how to take it. "Thanks? I don't wanna be a dick. I looked stuff up—" *Chest binder. God. Embarrassment.* "—but if I ever fuck up…"

"I'll tell you," James promised, laughing again. "Just down at the end, this house here."

Ryan's stomach dropped with disappointment, but then, a second later…

"If you wanted me to help you with the Grindr thing, by the way… or just have some tea for the road, if you're interested?" James offered.

Ryan hadn't been this interested in a long time, but he tried to play it cool. "You don't mind? Sure. I'd like that."

"Course I don't mind. I invited you, duh," James grumbled. "Park anywhere along here."

Once he did, James climbed out first to lead him to the house.

Ryan locked up the car behind him, the cool air bringing him back to his senses. He couldn't let himself get *totally* carried away.

They chatted about James's place—pointless chit-chat, of course—as they got their shoes and jackets off. James went to the kitchen side of the bachelor apartment to put the kettle on, and Ryan followed. That melted the tension, at least—until the moment James turned around again, leaning back against the counter. He was just a foot or two away from where Ryan leaned.

He could almost feel the heat from James's body. James's tongue darted along his lower lip.

James's voice was low but steady. "Do you want to kiss me?"

Ryan didn't know where the impulse had come from, but *fuck*, yes. He jerked his head in a quick nod. "D'you?"

James pushed himself away from the counter and toward Ryan, turning as he did. James stretched up onto his toes. One delicate hand settled on Ryan's shoulder, then trailed down his back. The other pulled him down into the kiss.

It was slow, hot, tentative…

And Ryan's barely-dormant interest was stirring awake again, his cock hardening and heart thumping. James's full lips slowly worked against his, their breathing sharp through their noses. James's stubble scraped Ryan's hand when Ryan cupped his cheek…

Then, James's body pressed against his, and Ryan instinctively pulled him in harder.

Oh, Jesus.

Business partners and friends with benefits? This wouldn't end well. For once in his carefully-planned and practical life, Ryan didn't care.

Fifteen

JAMES

THANK GOD HE'D ASKED THE QUESTION. RYAN WAS SO SWEET and careful to make sure he wasn't being weird or intrusive.

But it wasn't hard to read the way Ryan couldn't tear his eyes off him. Or the way he turned red and fidgeted with his jeans pocket when James told him how his packer worked. Or the way he was drawn magnetically close, leaning right next to him in the kitchen.

So he'd asked, flat-out, whether this gorgeous hunk wanted to kiss him. Apparently, the answer was *yes*, and that was all James needed.

James pressed into Ryan, trying not to let the heat get turned up too fast. *You can kiss a guy without going straight to sucking his dick,* he reminded himself, his heart pounding.

Their lips slid together, warm and wet and all tongues and teeth and lips; they were sucking, pressing, sliding…

He wasn't used to guys wanting to take it slow. Nobody wanted to join Grindr for clothed fun. Part of him felt like he *should* push this faster, show Ryan that he could still please him.

For now, he relaxed into the kiss, pressing his lips against Ryan's. They were the only part of him he'd gotten to touch so far that was soft.

Nope, now he'd found another. Ryan had a *great* ass. When James's hands ran down over it to pull him close and sidle up against him, the softest grunt slipped from Ryan's throat.

God. Did he know how hot he was? He had to. He was a good six inches taller than James, the kind of height guys wanted. He was broad-shouldered and muscled in the *pick you up and throw you against the mattress* way guys craved. And his face was radiant, his lips full, his jaw scruffy and stubbly…

He could be a fuckin' model, and he was here working as a carpenter in stupid Fredericton.

The comparison had begun, then. Already, James didn't feel like enough to catch his interest. But as Ryan pulled back from the kiss but kept his arms looped around his waist, hands flat on his back, James thought he *could* be.

"Jesus, you're a good kisser," Ryan murmured.

James smirked with pleasure, leaning up to press another kiss against Ryan's jaw. "So are you." With Ryan's back to the counter, he had him pinned there with his own smaller body. Neither of them were flinching back.

The chemistry between them was clear as day. Ryan's hand kept twitching toward his ass and thigh. He *so* wanted to be given permission to touch.

"I didn't think you were into me," Ryan breathed out after a second.

James winked. "If me staring at your ass for half an hour wasn't enough of a clue…"

"I was busy climbing a wall!"

"I was climbing the walls by the time you noticed, too." James winked, pleased when Ryan laughed. "So, now that we've gone and done this… may I remind us both how stupid it is?"

Ryan's hand ran up his back, eliminating any hope he had of protesting it. That broad hand running along his spine, cupping the back of his neck, then tangling in his hair? Oh, God, yes, he wanted more of that.

Ryan was saying something.

"Mmm?" James murmured, and Ryan laughed, repeating himself.

"That didn't stop us from this much."

"Not my fault you're so kissable," James informed Ryan with an airy shrug. "Or that I am." Ryan looked surprised, but laughed. "What? I am."

"Y-Yeah. You are." Ryan's tone of voice and nod were emphatic. He stared across the kitchen like he was composing himself.

James beamed. The compliment was so accepted. "Thanks."

The kettle clicked off and James let out a quick rush of breath. He slowly stepped back from Ryan's hold to give them both a second and some space. He quietly poured cups of tea.

It felt like the morning after, just seconds later.

Ryan barely met his eyes as he accepted the cup of tea. For a second, James started to worry. Then Ryan looked up again, almost through his lashes, and it occurred to him—he was *shy*.

Shit, a guy his size shy? And he'd thought Ryan couldn't get any more adorable… or fun to tease.

James beamed as he sipped his tea. "I left room for

cream," he murmured, letting innuendo slide through his tone.

Ryan choked and stared into his mug of black tea, eyes wide as he stifled his cough. It was obvious he didn't know how to handle a mouthy little bastard like James prided himself on being. "Cream, please."

Fuck that. James wasn't going to play damsel and wait for a big, strong, masc dude to sweep him off his feet. Ryan could try to keep up with him.

James flicked his fingers, his wrist limp, toward the fridge. "Soy cream in the fridge—"

"Yep," Ryan said quickly and moved over there, pouring some into his tea and stirring it.

James wanted to see what he did next. He wasn't disappointed—Ryan walked right back toward him, leaning right there again.

He still wants more. A shiver crawled down James's spine at the thought of all the things he wanted to do to Ryan—wanted Ryan to do to him. He very much agreed with the sentiment.

The sexual chemistry between them didn't abate for a second as they both sipped their cups of tea. Then, James leaned in and put down his mug, pressing a kiss below Ryan's ear. "You can kiss me like that again, you know."

Ryan slid his mug over the counter, not needing to be told twice.

Strong hands gripped his shoulders, turning him until he was back-on to the counter. That ripped body pressed him up against it, his biceps just right there as a hand ran up through his hair. The other hand ran down over his front toward his belt.

Best of all, Ryan's lips covered his, his breathing quick

and ragged. James ran his hand up Ryan's thighs. Ryan's breathing hitched when his palm ran over the bulge in his pants. He was unmistakably hard.

No surprise, after the gym and a car ride of teasing, and now kissing like porn stars.

James pushed past the moment of aching envy that he couldn't subtly push his own hardness directly into Ryan's thigh right now. It was sheltered under a layer of soft silicone.

The only sounds in the kitchen were rough breathing and rustles and smacks. Their breathing hitched together with each slow suck of lips on lips. Hands rustled on clothing as those hands *finally* ran down his thighs, then up his arms, feeling him up. Best of all, the wet smacks of lips on lips mingled with their rough breaths.

"I… *really* better get going, if this is a stupid idea," Ryan breathed out after a second. He was peeling his body away from James's. "But I don't think I'll need that Grindr profile, you know?"

James resisted the urge to press into that hard plane of masculinity in front of him and climb it like a tree. His chest heaved for breath. He hadn't been kissed like that in fucking *months*. As far as he was concerned, Ryan could do whatever the fuck he wanted to him now.

But he was trying to respect him, and James tried to remember that shouldn't be disappointing. Even better—he didn't want to hook up. Had that been some clumsy attempt to get closer?

"Yeah," James whispered after a second, then offered Ryan a cheeky grin. "It *would* be even more stupid if you stayed. Business partners."

"Business partners," Ryan agreed, clearing his throat and

straightening up as James did, too. "That—that list of things to build…"

"Already emailed you," James told him, trying not to think about that broad hand running up his spine to cup the back of his neck. His shivers were gone, though, very much replaced by the heat of arousal still roasting him.

As James walked Ryan to the door, talking chitchat about their business for the next week before that craft fair, it was the elephant in the room.

There was no way they could pretend this hadn't happened.

His shoes and jacket on, Ryan's eyes fell to James's lips for a long second when he opened the front door. Then he seemed to push past whatever thought had stopped him, swooping down to peck him on the lips.

"Night!" James grinned.

"Night." Ryan almost fled down the porch toward the car while James leaned in the doorway, grinning until his face hurt.

For a guy his size, Ryan could move nimbly when embarrassed.

Or when he wanted to pin him to the counter and kiss him like his life depended on it. Oh, James was gonna jack off to the memory of that one hot, *hot* fucking kiss for weeks.

"Wait, you just said you *kissed* him?"

"Fuck," Ryan groaned at the disbelieving, thrilled voice that came down the line. "Yes. Please don't tell the others."

Kevin laughed. "Dude. You know Cam texted me to say you're married to your phone?"

"He did?" Ryan was gonna slap him upside the head.

Kevin laughed. "God, I wish I could be there to see your lovey eyes."

"I do not have—now you're just making shit up."

"Maybe," Kevin snickered. "So, you're calling for advice? Why?"

"God knows. It seemed like a good idea five minutes ago," Ryan grumbled, both of them laughing. "Just confirmation that it's stupid, I guess."

"It *is* stupid, mixing business and pleasure, but plenty of people do it. Married couples run businesses."

Ryan's cheeks flushed with heat as he turned on his heel, pacing the other way through his workshop. "That's different."

"Mm. It is," Kevin acknowledged, his voice more serious now. "I get the whole *coworkers, can't do this* thing," he assured Ryan. After all, he was quietly dating another pro hockey player. That was a pretty big taboo to break in Canadian sports culture. "But seriously, that just means you *get* each other, too. I mean, you've worked with plenty of other guys on the job, right? It's not just proximity."

"It's not," Ryan agreed. He'd been captivated by James from across the room, before they'd even spoken. There had just been a spark. He couldn't say *that*, though. Kevin would make fun of him. "He's not in a stable position right now, though. We need to get income coming in. That's more important for him right now—stability."

"Very mature," Kevin praised him, and he was only half-teasing. "So, when does that happen?"

"We've got a stall at the fair the day after tomorrow. Saturday."

"And have you seen him since the kiss?"

"No," Ryan groaned. To be fair, he'd been absorbed in work. He'd had long days on the job before coming home to finish the inventory pieces James had instructed him to make. "He's coming over today to help finish stuff that's already built. Paint and sanding, that kind of work."

"Ahhh. And you're worried about that awkward moment," Kevin filled in. "Just push through it, man. If he's stressed about this, too, he won't wanna waste time, either."

"Right," Ryan agreed. "Get through this show first and then see where we're at."

"This is the first real market test," Kevin agreed. "You know, Floyd or Jackson would be able to help more with that."

"No, I'm confident that what he said about the market is right," Ryan told Kevin. "He knows his shit, business-wise."

"I meant for moral support. Being a business owner is stressful. Like being a freelancer. A lot of us technically are."

Ryan had learned more than he'd ever thought he'd know about pro hockey since Kevin moved to Toronto. "Oh. Yeah, we're having a barbecue with everyone on Sunday, after the show."

"With James there?"

"Yeah. Oh, shit, I haven't invited him."

Kevin laughed. "Well done," he teased. "Invite him tonight, and then just focus on the show. And, man?"

"Yeah?"

"I'm glad you told me. Seriously, man, I haven't heard you talk so much in ages. He's good for you to be around, in whatever way. Don't keep him a secret."

"I won't," Ryan promised. "Like you did with Matty—"

"That was different," Kevin hotly retorted, and Ryan laughed.

"Right. Of course," Ryan smirked. "But I'm not telling everyone what's going on until *I* know."

"Smart," Kevin told him. "Give him some space to figure things out, too, huh?"

Ryan nodded to himself, then remembered Kevin couldn't see. "Yep."

"Awesome. Let me know how it goes, then, huh?"

"I will," Ryan promised. "Thanks. Good luck with the media training!"

"Anytime. Catch you later."

Ryan let out a breath, his heart thumping with nerves. Any minute now, James would be here. Suddenly Ryan was worried about how he looked in his work clothes—torn jeans, sawdust-covered plaid shirt, wood stain streaked along his clothes...

But it was too late to worry about that, because that was definitely a knock he'd just heard on the door. "Come in!"

James poked his head in, then grinned. "Whoa, someone's been busy."

When James entered a room, it seemed to light up. He had that kind of bright presence and energy around him that was impossible to miss. It was one of the reasons Ryan smiled so much around him.

"Yep," Ryan agreed, gesturing around. Some pieces were finished, but a lot of stuff needed staining, and he'd been waiting for a good, warm, dry day.

They'd finally had it, with no time to spare. The show setup was tomorrow night. These had to get their final coat of stain so they'd be dry in time.

"Ready to work?" Ryan asked. James had worn that same cute outfit—dark jeans and a plaid shirt—that he had on his first time visiting. These must be his work clothes.

"Yep. Your turn to order me around!" James grinned.

Ryan abruptly remembered—or his body did, or both—that it was their first time seeing each other in person since the kisses in James's kitchen.

"Great," Ryan clapped his hands together. He pulled open the sliding window-doors along the back of the building. He'd gotten off work at three after an early shift. It was early enough in the day that they could get a few more hours of fresh air and sunshine in here.

"Breezy," James commented.

Ryan remembered how cold James got. "Are you fine with that?"

"Better than getting a paint high," James laughed. "I'm

fine." He spotted the paint brushes and grabbed one, tapping it against his palm. "Just show me what to do."

It was easy instructing him. He listened well and paid attention when Ryan told him how to paint along the grain to highlight the character of the wood.

Better yet, he actually followed those instructions. That gave him a big leg up on half the apprentices they saw at the company.

Ryan was able to leave him to staining the wine bottle holders while he sanded down the sets of coasters. "So," Ryan spoke up when they had a comfortable moment, "how was your week?"

"Great," James told him. "Got our website almost set up."

"Oh, shit. Sorry. I haven't had a chance to look yet," Ryan winced. James had been texting him updates, but he hadn't texted back much. Combined with what they'd last done together, James might be thinking he was withdrawing.

"No problem," James answered. "This is all more important."

"I'm sure it looks great. Show me after this is done," Ryan told him, and James brightened up.

"Will do. How about yours?"

Aside from work and then more work on this, Ryan hadn't had much time for anything fun. He entertained James with anecdotes from the job site. A terribly misdirected nail gun had almost taken out a stack of windows that day.

"That must be taking a toll, all this extra work," James frowned. "You should teach me the basics so I can do… you know, the grunt work."

Actually, that sounded perfect. "Really?" Ryan asked to be sure. "It *is* tough sometimes."

James eyed him. "You think I'm allergic to hard work?" he teased, but he was a little affronted. He probably thought Ryan didn't think he was manly enough for it or something. Ryan had read about that online.

"Nah. You're here," Ryan gestured around with the brush, almost splashing stain on James. "Oops."

"You painting me? I'll paint you," James threatened, his eyes crinkling in another of those adorable smiles.

Ryan laughed. "We *can't* get into a stain fight."

"Agreed," James smirked. "No time, no extra supplies. You're so damn practical."

"So are you, Mr. I Track Everything In A Spreadsheet, Probably Even My Breakfasts…"

James turned red.

"What? No," Ryan exclaimed, his belly rumbling with his laugh.

"I *once* tracked my meal intake, just to optimize—oh, shut up," James laughed. He was flustered.

Oops. Ryan really wanted to kiss him. He shivered and quickly moved around to the other side of the shoe rack he was working on. He focused on staining the rods along the back. "See? Nerd."

"I'm proud of it."

"I need a nerd keeping me on track. Obviously. Look at all this!" Ryan gestured around the workshop.

He knew for damn certain he would have worked on *maybe* a piece a week, if the right people had asked him to. With James texting him every morning to see what he was working on that day, dropping off supplies, and telling him his lumber budget, he had direction and focus.

"Damn straight," James agreed, dipping his brush in thinner. "There. What next?"

Ryan shook his head. James worked well *and* fast, without the lazy coffee breaks of half his coworkers, and even himself. "Stop putting me to shame."

"You have more surface area."

"I sure do," Ryan laughed and patted his chest. The humor was not lost on James, who cracked up. "But you're pretty flexible. Jesus, the day after climbing!"

"You couldn't move?" James laughed. "That's a problem, yeah."

"I kinda want to go again, though," Ryan admitted. "It was weirdly… addictive?"

"Yes! I know, right?" James enthused, lighting up. That was it. He could just let James talk away now. "And you should see the outdoor climbing here."

"Mm?"

"Southern New Brunswick. There's nothing around at all except some good routes. Well, we don't have any tricky routes exactly, nothing graded above a 5.13, but we're working on it. There's a group of local climbers—I go out with them sometimes," James paused to explain. "We're planning to climb over Thanksgiving. And I might go alone, too. It's technically dangerous, but you can belay yourself, too."

"Oh?"

"Yeah, it's not for amateurs," James warned. "There's a lot that can go wrong. You anchor yourself and you can use a regular grigri, like the locking device you used. Or you can use one specially made for it."

Ryan's brows pinched with worry. All he could see was James getting hurt out there in the wilderness with nobody to help. "I can drive down for part of the weekend," he offered. "If you need a partner."

James's expression lit up. "Would you? I'm sure my dad

would like to have you over. I'm not sure which house I'm going to for… what dinner… but we could sort that out."

"My parents will be disappointed if I miss supper," Ryan chuckled. He hadn't missed that—divorced parents, then. That had to be rough. "But I could drop by, if you want."

"Ahh, right." James smiled as he started picking up stray pieces of wood and tidying up around Ryan, helping clean up. "Your parents get on with you, then?"

"Pretty well, yeah." Ryan smiled. "I'm lucky."

"Mine… sort of do. Oh, you'll see," James rolled his eyes as he shrugged. "Whatever. It's fake-turkey dinner and a good chance to climb."

Near the end of their work session, Ryan remembered his conversation with Kevin. James was almost finished screwing the hooks into the front door shelves and key racks when Ryan turned to him.

"Hey, speaking of suppers, are you free tomorrow?"

"I could be," James smiled, looking up at him. "Why?"

"I often have Sunday barbecues with my buddies. You know Cam, Jackson, and Thomas?"

James chuckled. "Yeah. I've heard of their little…" he trailed off.

"Commune?" Ryan supplied with a laugh. The three brothers owned houses next to each other with a shared backyard, and all three had boyfriends who lived with them. That made them a novelty. No doubt James *had* heard of them. "You can say it."

"You said it, not me!" James chuckled. "Yeah, I've met them at the auctions a couple times."

"You wanna come to a barbecue tomorrow? They're dying to meet you. As—as my friend, and business partner," Ryan added, his cheeks burning. He didn't want it to sound like he'd been gossiping about kissing James the way he... well, he had. Or that he thought they were... more than friends.

James was blushing, too. "Yeah, I'd like that. Just tell me where and when."

"I'll text you the address," Ryan promised, but he was already smiling. He couldn't wait for James to meet everyone.

Then, James took a breath, looking like he was preparing for a less pleasant conversation. "Have you told them about me being trans?"

"God, no," Ryan quickly said, then caught his breath. "I mean, not that it's bad. Just, I read it was rude."

James was chuckling again, and that look in his eyes was unmistakably fond. Ryan wished he could see that look directed at him more often. "How much *did* you read?" he grinned.

Ryan cleared his throat, embarrassed now. "Only the basics. A lot of stuff said *ask the person you know because everyone's different*, so it wasn't... terribly helpful."

"Still," James smiled. "Thanks. Yeah. I'm not *hiding* it, but it's nice not to have it be the first thing people know about me."

That made complete sense to Ryan. In fact, that was exactly how he treated his sexuality, especially on the job. It took him a second to wrap his brain around the wisdom of that sentence. "Yeah. Yeah, I get it."

James nodded thoughtfully, then smiled again. "Thanks for inviting me, too. I was worried that we... you know... screwed up."

"No, no," Ryan quickly chuckled. "Just, with this coming up—"

"Better to focus on it, yeah—"

"Yep, distractions—"

"Yeah."

They stopped fumbling to agree with each other. Ryan's heart skipped a beat as he realized how close James was standing, one hand full of brushes. "Sink's there," Ryan mumbled after a moment.

"Cool."

James rinsed them off while Ryan stood back to check their work and make sure they weren't missing anything.

Ryan wasn't sure how long it had been. Time flew by with idle chatting, not to mention teaching James all the basic finishing steps of his work. "Want to come in for supper?" Ryan asked.

"Sure," James smiled. "If you don't mind."

"Course I don't mind," Ryan didn't miss the chance to parrot, grinning. "That's why I asked, duh."

"Jerk," James stuck out his tongue and walked ahead of Ryan to his house.

Ryan laughed, leaving the full-length windows open to air out the workshop while the pieces dried. Whether or not they were making out, it was just *easy* to be around James.

"I found a vegan pizza at the store. I've been keeping it in my freezer for this occasion."

James brightened up so much that Ryan kind of wanted to hug him. How infrequently did people take his diet into consideration or forget it?

As he pushed open the back door of the house and Ryan followed him in, James caught the way Ryan was watching him. "Yeah, a lot of people don't think about that. My parents included."

"Sorry," Ryan frowned. "That's shitty. Bathroom's that way if you want to wash up first."

He had to take a second after James stepped through the door and closed it just to draw a breath and let it out.

Whether or not they were sticking to being business partners, James's presence was intoxicating. Sooner or later, that was going to be a problem unless he got himself under control now.

CHAPTER
Seventeen

JAMES

It was stupid early to be awake, but the second James's eyes opened, he jolted to life.

He had so much to do today, and he couldn't miss any of his buses.

"Shower," he mumbled to himself. The sooner he hit the shower, the sooner he could fool himself into feeling awake.

James started the kettle on his way past the kitchen. He was glad that after Ryan had dropped him off last night, he'd thought to fill it with water.

And there it was: the prickle of heat that glided through his body at the thought of Ryan. Driving him home, absent-mindedly running his hand back through his hair. Biting his lip and nodding as he listened to James talk. Looking over at him like he was the only guy in the world.

James shivered, shutting the bathroom door behind him and stripping his boxers off.

No harm in letting his memory keep going.

Those big, roughened hands around the steering wheel.

He didn't have to imagine what they'd feel like running up his hips and sides to his chest. He remembered being pressed up against the counter, a strong hand gently running up to his cheek to cup it.

And the way Ryan kissed. Shit, he was good. He was slow and intense at first, taking his time with each suck of James's lip and each grind of their bodies. It was all James could do not to rub himself up against him with desperation.

Fuck, how good would he be in bed?

James gave up on the idea of not jerking off to Ryan *every single morning* that week. The hot water hitting his body made him moan his appreciation. He tugged the shower curtain across so fast he almost ripped it off its rings.

He needed to feel Ryan's body blanketing his in bed, Ryan's hands tangling in his fingers, catching his hands and pulling them up above his head, Ryan's hard cock pressing into his hip...

He stepped forward until the pulsing jets of warm water hit his face. Sheets of water coursed over his flat chest and hard-won abs, and between his legs.

Jesus. Ryan had no idea the effect he had on him, did he? James had hinted that he wouldn't mind being fucked into the wall by him, but Ryan had backed off.

Sensibly, his brain reminded him with that damn phrase *business partners* once again. But this wasn't the time for practicality. He was allowed to imagine whatever he damn well pleased.

Ryan tossed sheets of plywood like they were paper. He could heft two-by-fours and twist them around without thinking twice...

And when he worked shirtless. Shit, those were the *best* times to visit. Sometimes he opened the workshop door to the sight of Ryan hammering nails into a backboard or running a strip of wood through the table saw. Sawdust stuck to his pecs, sweat trickling down his back into his jeans...

James braced himself against the wall with one hand, pushing his hips forward into the jet of water. The pressure of the day ahead of him was already weighing on him; he had no time to waste.

He let his imagination jump forward, pulling out the hottest images he could manage as he closed his fingers around his cock. It was easy to feel and see when he was hard. The pinkness poked between his thumb and index finger as he jerked slowly—at first.

Ryan's lips dragged along the hair of his inner thigh, his tongue a hot, wet line of *teasing* all the way up to James's cock. His eyes sparkled with their usual wicked glint.

Ryan's fingers trailed around his nipples, finding the skin with full erotic sensation. He'd be good at that. He'd use it to make James's back arch off the bed as he threw his head back and moaned.

Ryan's cock pushed at him, hard and thick and hot. Ryan buried himself inside James's body with a sharp thrust of his hips until their cries mingled.

Or maybe Ryan would whimper when James's slick fingers circled his hole and slid inside. The shallow thrusts of his hips would feel like riding a barely-leashed hurricane, pushing him teasingly on and on toward the edge.

Ryan would be tight around him as James slid into him. His breath would catch in his throat. His eyes would glaze over as he pushed his face into the bed and his hips up for him.

Fuck, the number of things he wanted to feel and have

Ryan make him feel. The hot feeling of bare skin on skin, the groaning and grunting, no matter who was on top. James could feel their bodies working together to hit the perfect spots until they both shivered with bliss.

James's nails scraped the tile wall of the shower. His knees buckled and he came hard, thrusting into his hand and the water. He hissed at the sudden overwhelming heat rushing through him.

"R-Ryan… Oh, *fucking yes*," he moaned, his hips thrusting in quick, shuddery jerks. He let his mind fixate again on Ryan's body pressing hard against his, and how fucking close they'd been to ripping each other's clothes off right there in the kitchen.

When consciousness started to return, so did practicality, and he gasped under his breath. No time to waste. As far as quick and dirty showers went, he'd just gotten the dirty done. Speed was of the essence now.

Minutes later, his hair only half-dry, James jogged out the door, his backpack and game face on. Ryan worked until four today. Setup ran from six-thirty to eight-thirty tonight at the craft fair hall.

He had a long list of small but important things to buy—sticky-tack, more sheets of price stickers, zip-ties, the works.

On his way past, James opened his mailbox on instinct. A distinctive white envelope made him grimace, but he pulled it out anyway.

The return address was his credit card company.

When he made it down the street to the bus stop, he fumbled his earbuds into place. He tore open the envelope and glanced at the numbers.

He didn't need his spreadsheets in front of him to tell him

they weren't good. As much fun as it was to spend so much time around Ryan, James's mood sank as reality sank in again. This whole thing had to pay off.

CHAPTER
Eighteen

RYAN

"James and Ryan, from Hart Wood."

Ryan still smiled when he said their business name. James had been so damn proud of it that Ryan had said yes. Even when Ryan had tried to encourage him to include his own name, James had refused. The wordplay was too good to resist.

"Ah, I've got you boys here." The woman standing at the entrance desk checked off a piece of paper. She handed them both white lanyards. "Your table number is sixteen. Bring these tomorrow so our entrance girls don't charge you admission if you go out to your car for anything."

James took the lanyards and jerked his chin in a quick nod. "Thanks."

"If you need anything to set up, let us know," she told them. "I'm Kate."

"Thanks, Kate," Ryan chimed in with a polite nod. "We should be fine."

As he and James carried their first load of stuff to their

table, Ryan's heart was thumping with nerves. He'd never done this kind of thing before in any capacity, and he had no idea what to expect.

James was walking tall and confident, though. Apparently, he'd manned booths for his small business incubator, so he knew how they were set up.

And he attended craft fairs, which didn't surprise Ryan at all, but still delighted him.

"This one here," James directed him toward a table in the center area.

Ryan glanced around as he set down his tub of signage.

"It's a pretty good spot," James added as an afterthought. He leaned over to check the names of the tables nearby. "I like it."

"Good. I'll start grabbing the heavy stuff first."

James nodded his approval. "Good plan. We'll get that set up first and arrange everything around it."

Each time Ryan came back from his car, James had made more progress on the setup.

Shit. It looked like a real business now.

They were hoping for a thousand dollars in profit once the table fee and expenses were covered. According to James, that was actually a reasonable expectation for a two-day show with a short Sunday. Only trouble was, James said they couldn't predict which days or times would be the best sellers. Sometimes you stood behind the table and didn't sell a thing. Other times, you couldn't keep up with demand.

Of course, they hoped for the latter. Ryan hoped they would sell out their inventory. James seemed to be trying to keep his expectations reasonable, though. He wouldn't engage with Ryan when Ryan said anything like that.

James noticed him standing in front of the table, admiring the banner he'd gotten from *somewhere* at the last minute. "Look good?"

Ryan could read the nervousness in James's eyes as he took a breather for a second to gauge Ryan's reactions. Ryan smiled. "It's… awesome. Just feels real all of a sudden."

"Yeah," James chuckled. "I know what you mean. We're doing this."

Ryan was already in the hole for the materials, website setup costs, and table setup, but hopefully a grant would repay some of those costs. James had told him it would take time to hear back on that. Ryan let him handle those details. Just in case, they'd budgeted as if they wouldn't get any help.

Well, not *they*, like he had a hand in it. He put in his sweat equity, and James did all those spreadsheet things to earn his fifty percent.

"Right," Ryan said, clapping his hands together. Enough talk, more action. They only had a short window to set up. "It looks like you have the table almost ready to go. Where do you want these things?"

They went back and forth on where to put the largest items—behind the table or beside it. Finally, they agreed on the right angle to catch people's eye without blocking in the next-door stallholders.

Next, they settled the banner position along the front of the table. It was easy after that to set up smaller items— jewelry boxes on a stepstool, serving trays tilted just so, wine bottle holders behind birdhouses. Eventually, Ryan let James handle the positioning. Every time he placed an item just so, James would fix it—and James's setup *did* look better.

"Don't stop," James encouraged him after a minute, glancing at him.

Ryan laughed. "I thought I'd save you the trouble of fixing my bad eye for aesthetics."

"Dude, no, you *made* this stuff. You don't have a bad eye," James shook his head.

"Then you show it off better than me. Either way, that's it, isn't it?" Ryan smiled. "It looks awesome. Come see."

James came around the table to stand by him, then took several paces back to see the table from a distance. "Damn."

Ryan glanced at James to see his first glimpse of the table setup from afar, then smiled at the pride that swelled his chest. He was so cute all the time, but especially right now.

"And right on time. It's eight now," James told him after digging out his phone for a few photos of the setup.

Despite himself, Ryan was tired out. "We better get some sleep," he nodded. "I'll give you a lift home."

"That'd be awesome, thanks."

James never stopped thanking him for the rides home. It was sweet but totally unnecessary. Ryan wasn't going to drive home and leave him to wait hours for the next shitty city bus.

On the way back to his house, James was quiet. Probably worn out, Ryan figured. Fair enough—so was he. It had already been weeks of preparing for this weekend, and the ones coming up afterward. Keeping up with his own day job took enough energy, too.

When they reached James's house, Ryan pulled over in front of it and looked over with a smile.

As always, James thanked him again as he opened the car door and slid out.

"No problem. I'll be here at seven on the dot." Ryan leaned down and over to look at him. "We'll make sure we're set up over there, grab Tim's, and settle down for the day."

They'd been over the plan before, but Ryan just wanted to make sure. He was craving Timbits now, too, but that could wait until the morning.

"Bingo. Seven," James promised with a laugh. "See you tomorrow!"

Ryan realized only when he was pulling into his own driveway that his chest was aching. He wasn't ready to say good night yet.

James was just easy to spend time with. That was all.

"How can I help you?" Before Ryan approached the shopper, James swept in from the other side of the table, beaming.

"I was just wondering how much these were."

Ever-patient, never mentioning the price tags in a way that would embarrass them, James gave the prices. He started to chat about what they'd seen the customer looking at—wine bottle holders.

Ryan stepped back to let him in, keeping an overview eye on their table.

It worked out well: James made first contact. He drew people in to chat with his charming and, like it or not, flirta-tious smile. That was just the way James was around every-one, smiley and enthusiastic.

That, and very flamboyant. It made Ryan twitch slightly with nerves when James approached the older guys or the more guarded ones with girlfriends. But women loved the attention and ate up the cute little guy bouncing over to them with a *how-you-doing* or *great-fair-today*.

The morning had been slow, but business and sales were

picking up at about the same rate. Ryan had to try not to count up the money in the box in his excitement. There was a float, after all, and this wasn't profit—just gross income.

Still, it was a good sign. They weren't all alone, like the three jewelry makers across the aisle with very similar product lines. James had cleverly chosen some pieces that the other woodworkers here sold. Others, like the key holders, nobody else seemed to be selling today.

And they'd already sold their largest item, the folding backyard table. James had positively glowed as he took payment for that item and helped the customers get it out to their car.

Ryan was starting to see the appeal of backyard furniture, but James had insisted they keep it smaller for now. There were already several patio furniture makers in the area. Their rustic hand-woven benches were gorgeous but hard for people to fit into their cars.

"How much is this?"

Ryan stepped forward when a customer made eye contact with him and James was still busy. "Fifteen dollars for one, two for twenty-five," he answered, smiling. He wasn't as adorable and dorky as James, but *could* be good at customer service, too.

"Great. Are you a new business?"

"Yes. This is our first official event," Ryan told her. She looked like a middle-aged mom shopping for presents for her friends.

"Oh! Good for you."

"Thank you. Is there anyone you're shopping for in particular today, or treating yourself?" Ryan asked with a smile, echoing one of James's lines.

"My girlfriends. One of them is *so* hard to shop for, you know? One of those people who buys whatever she wants!"

The product solution was obvious—Ryan directed her toward the wine bottle holders. Then, James came wiggling in. James easily took over the conversation, laughing about girlfriends and wine. He played the gay best friend to a tee while Ryan took payment.

They worked seamlessly together. James was good at sensing when he had rapport with customers and vice versa. Passing change back and forth when needed kept them within arm's-reach of each other. They soon developed a system for making sure any customers who came to their table were acknowledged as quickly as possible.

James was on Ryan's left side before long, mired in a conversation about reclaimed wood. "We have to be careful which sources we choose, of course," James explained, as Ryan gazed at him. He'd listened to everything Ryan had idly discussed in the workshop while developing products. He was a little information sponge, and it never ceased to amaze Ryan.

Still talking, James reached around him and tapped his right shoulder to indicate that there was a potential customer that way. Ryan jolted back to attention; James had the conversation covered.

He approached the next customer with an easier smile. The nerves from the first few hours were gone. It was just exciting now to talk to people face-to-face about his work.

And the compliments—hell, they'd be flattering for anyone. He was used to his work being buried within joists and walls, painted over, and only noticed when it was done badly.

Now, the technical quality of his work was front and center, and he hadn't fallen down on it.

"Oh, look who we have here."

Roger was there with a couple of his buddies—the ones who made Ryan's hackles rise. They had stopped by the job site before. They often took Roger out for lunch or headed down to the States with him on Friday afternoons.

They weren't the type he'd expected to see at the nice community craft fair. There was nothing *wrong* with them, exactly; they hadn't said anything shitty, but Ryan knew their type. They were the ones who would, if anyone.

"Hello!" James greeted, smiling at them, undeterred. "Oh, you know Ryan?"

"We work together," Ryan said simply, smiling at Roger and leaning in to clap Roger's shoulder in greeting. "Good to see you. Never mind me, what are you doing here?"

Roger was watching James for a second before he looked back at Ryan. "Thought we'd come check out the competition."

"Competition?" Ryan feigned ignorance, but he felt James stiffen beside him.

"Oh, you didn't hear? I have a regular stall at the north market now."

Ryan blinked at him. "Oh, I had no idea. I went last week, but I didn't see you."

It was true—on a quick morning scout of the place, no sign of Roger, but there *was* an empty table with his name on it.

"Good for you," Ryan added. "I had no idea you were planning to start a business too."

"It's a shame, we could have worked together," Roger

added. "I'm Roger," he added, introducing himself to James with a quick nod.

"James."

"You his… business partner? Employee?"

"Partner," Ryan supplied before James could answer, smiling. "I do the building, he does literally everything else."

"That seems like the easy way out," Roger teased, and Ryan picked up on that patronizing tone. Roger thought less of everyone who wasn't built like a linebacker. He wanted to tell James not to take it personally.

James had cooled off, his eyebrow raising for a second. "You do it all solo?"

"Just about," Roger answered, his chin tilted in that bragging manner.

"Did the market close early today, then?"

Ryan bit back his laugh as Roger eyed James. His coworker had to admit, "No. I left a buddy there to come check out what's here."

Oh, James saw just as well as Ryan did the way Roger was looking at what he was selling, and for how much. James looked like he wanted to say something, but Ryan just smiled.

Not worth it, man. He'll never follow through.

"Better get going and leave you to it," Roger finally said after an awkward second. He shook Ryan's hand and clapped his arm. "See you at work Monday." He looked at James, his lip curling slightly. He didn't offer his hand.

"See you Monday," Ryan answered with a bland smile. He watched the three of them until they were a few stalls away.

James's jaw was tight as he watched them away, then looked at Ryan.

Ryan nodded toward the customers who were approaching with an apologetic look.

"Tell me later," James said simply, then turned back to them with a bright smile. "Hello!"

Not for the first time, Ryan was grateful that James was so damn good with people.

CHAPTER
Nineteen

JAMES

IT WASN'T HARD FOR JAMES TO FEEL ROGER'S DISLIKE FOR Ryan, let alone for him. The two looked like the kind of guys who barely got on at work and didn't outside of it.

Still, James shelved the incident until the last stragglers had been ushered out of the fair hall.

"Twenty-forty-sixty-eight-hundred-twenty-forty-sixty—" James mumbled. He was counting the thick stack of twenties that they'd pulled and hidden under the cash tray.

Once he finished reporting the totals to Ryan, Ryan counted to make sure he hadn't made any mistakes. James pulled out his phone to enter the numbers into his spreadsheet.

"So?" Ryan asked, the barely-veiled hope simmering away. They both knew their gross sales figure was good.

"We made about six hundred each."

Even James was stunned. He'd been hoping for five hundred each after expenses, after the weekend was done. If tomorrow gave them half the sales they were hoping for…

Wow.

"That's great, isn't it?" Ryan's eyes were bright, like he was waiting for James to give him permission to get excited.

James laughed, reaching out to high-five Ryan. "That's fucking awesome," he corrected him.

Ryan's answering laugh was rich.

It was six, just about time for supper, but James was already ready for bed. The long day dealing with a crowd had energized him, but he still had to recharge and get ready for tomorrow. There was a half-day of this, plus the barbecue with Ryan's friends.

"Right," Ryan nodded after a moment and locked up the cash box, hefting it under one arm. "I'll give you a ride home, huh?"

"Thanks," James nodded, pulling out his phone to check the spreadsheet numbers again. "I'm just gonna Netflix and chill tonight."

Ryan was quiet, which wasn't unusual. When James glanced up, he caught a flicker of something in his eyes. It was gone as fast as that. "Right," Ryan agreed. "I'll just sleep, like, twelve hours tonight."

James laughed. "Crowds take it out of you, don't they?"

He'd seen Ryan's best attempts to interact with people. While Ryan had done fine, it was clearly more of an effort for him. Despite his size, Ryan was actually quite shy. James wasn't sure how many people had figured that out.

"Yeah," Ryan sighed and rolled his eyes. "And I wanna get those custom orders written down so I can start on them Monday night."

James beamed. He'd almost forgotten about those—a few people had wanted custom-made pieces, and he'd taken down those details. That looked like a good revenue stream, too. "Right! Cool. Let me know if you need me to pick anything up for them."

"Will do," Ryan smiled as they headed for the door.

They had to stop for a minute to chat with Kate about the day, but a couple of stall vendors with similar products who had been positioned too close together ambushed her. James let her go and went out to Ryan's car with him.

"So..." James finally spoke up when they were in the car. "Those guys earlier?"

"Oh! Roger. I almost forgot," Ryan admitted. "He's just kind of an asshole. He doesn't like that I'm friends with our boss, but he has a shitty work ethic. I'm surprised he's gotten this far if he's trying to copy me."

James's heart jolted. "Copy—you think he's taking your designs?"

"He can try," Ryan said simply, drawing James's gaze as he started up the car. That handsome face and chiseled jaw looked calm. Ryan wasn't even clenching his teeth to say it. "He's a good woodworker. He'll go far if he does."

James nodded slowly. "Do we need to be looking at patents? Can we patent them?"

"I wouldn't bother," Ryan said and shrugged. "He's not even at his own stall, what, two weeks? Three weeks after starting it?"

James saw his point. But the way Roger had looked at him... *that* rubbed him the wrong way, too. He had to ask. "Does he know about you?"

"Yeah. He's overheard," Ryan muttered, frowning as he drummed his fingers. "So his buddies probably do, too. I wouldn't worry about them, if you are," he added. "I don't think they're the hillbilly type."

James relaxed. "Okay." Still, the thought of Ryan working with some guy who acted like he was allergic to the gays made him roll his eyes. "Just dicks?"

"Just dicks," Ryan agreed, nodding.

James breathed out a chuckle, staying quiet until they got back to his house.

"Thanks for the ride," he told Ryan at last, leaning in to hug him once his seatbelt was unbuckled. "Great job today."

Ryan seemed surprised. He laughed and raised his arms to squeeze him in an awkward hug. He almost beeped the car horn with his elbow. "You, too. We did great."

"We did," James agreed with a cheery grin. With his credit card statement on the fridge, he was *itching* for the Monday bank run. He'd have to be patient for a little longer.

After Saturday's rush of shoppers, Sunday morning felt mellow, and James didn't mind that. The hours passed fast, the fair open just until three. It wasn't until about one that customers started to pack the place again.

This time, without the desperation to prove the viability of the business, he felt more laid-back. He chatted with whoever came by. His goal was to firmly establish them as a great, new, all-local business to support.

Better yet, nobody seemed to recognize him from his old workplace. He even saw a couple of shoppers who he *knew* had walked away from his till back at the store. It was amazing what happened when he didn't have a girl's name pinned to his chest.

They sold out of wine bottle holders first, and then the stepping stool sold. The tacky signs were almost all gone when he stepped away for a bite to eat. By the time he came back, Ryan gave him a thumbs-up and pointed out the empty spot where the small hanging shelf had been standing on the table.

By the last hour of shopping, their inventory was even lower than James had been hoping.

"I guess we don't need to do a clearance sale." Ryan leaned over and grinned when the last few customers started heading for the doors.

James laughed. "Don't even try," he warned Ryan. "That'll cut into our profit margin. Everything here will sell next week."

Ryan held up his hands and widened his eyes. "You're the expert! I wouldn't dream of it." He hummed as he pulled out bins to start packing up. He was clearly on a high from the successful sale, even if he wasn't enthusing.

James laughed under his breath, then beamed when Kate came around.

"Hello! Wow, you two made out like bandits! People loved it, huh?"

James's face just about split with his grin. "They did! I'm so relieved," he admitted to Kate. "I mean, I knew it's all good work, but... competition, and our first show..."

"This was your *very first*?" Kate exclaimed. "Wow. Very professional."

God, that was a relief to hear. James leaned in for a hug when she did. "Thank you *so* much. It's been a long few weeks."

"And you chose a smart cookie for your partner," Kate winked at Ryan after hugging James.

Ryan smiled back at her, reaching out for a handshake.

He was blushing. "I know I did. Thank you for the opportunity."

Oh my God. She doesn't think...? James bit back his smile.

"Of course! I have your contact details—I'll be in touch before my next fair."

"We'd love that," James smiled.

Other stallholders came over to chat as they all packed up, the lights turned up and the doors locked shut to keep stray shoppers out. James was high on their results himself, itching to check the cash box again.

"Shall we head back to mine and settle up before the barbecue?" Ryan suggested when they hauled the last bin out to his car and leaned against it to catch their breath. Well, James did the leaning, while Ryan looked like he hadn't broken a sweat.

"I'd love to," James beamed back at him. When they were in the car, he had to chuckle. "I think she thought we were—"

"Yeah." Ryan laughed along with him, his eyes crinkling as he gazed over at him. "I wonder how much we'll get that."

"Does it bother you?" James asked. He kind of hoped not, but either way, he had to know.

"Let them assume what they want. They will anyway," Ryan told him.

James smiled again. "Very wise," he teased as Ryan drove them back to his house. He bounced the cash box on his knees.

"Can't sit still, can you?" Ryan said, smiling.

"Fuck, no. This is way better than I ever expected," James admitted. "If only the bank were open today."

"I'll drive you there tomorrow morning, if you want," Ryan offered.

James brightened up. He hadn't been eagerly anticipating walking to the bank with that much in cash on him. "Would you?"

"Of course. I gotta deposit mine, too. Your house is almost on the way."

Sort of, if one ignored the detour through a few neighborhoods and an annoying one-way street. James didn't call him out on it, just chuckled. "Great. Thanks."

"You can stop thanking me for rides," Ryan grumbled. "Of course I'm gonna give you a ride whenever you need it."

James wanted *so* badly to make an innuendo-filled pun about that, but he bit his tongue.

A second later, Ryan's cheeks turned red, and James snickered. He wasn't the only one still feeling the tension between them. It flared when there weren't crowds of people around to distract them. Packing up with Ryan had reminded James of that very physical, raw energy he seemed to carry with him. It had been all he could do not to react to it in public.

"You're awful," Ryan laughed, but he didn't mean it. His eyes were crinkled, his hand running back through his hair as he watched the road.

James watched the hair wrapping around and sliding between those thick fingers and imagined his own fingers tangling in it instead. "Mmm," he agreed. "I've been told."

"Are you gonna behave around my friends?"

"Probably not," James deadpanned, making Ryan crack another smile. "But, yeah, of course. I might be a little high off how that went, though."

"Me, too," Ryan assured him, finally glancing over at him. His gaze was warm. "It's good to see you smile so much."

"I always smile!" James protested.

Ryan hummed under his breath and looked ahead again.

James went still, his heart hammering. What was Ryan thinking? He seemed like the type not to say unless prompted, so he waited a second, then hummed. "Hm?"

"The more you worry, the more you smile."

Oh. Shit.

James looked out the window for a second. Yeah, he was positive in general and optimistic, but Ryan was dead right. It was a bit of a defense mechanism. It applied to placating a screaming parent or placating angry, drunk men.

It was just rare for people to notice that.

He swallowed hard, then nodded. "Yeah. We all have our habits."

Ryan's broad hand squeezed his shoulder, making him look over at him. They were at Ryan's house and Ryan was backing into the driveway. He looked over his shoulder, then at James as he let go of him and pulled the parking brake up.

James didn't say anything, his smile wavering.

"I'm glad I picked you."

Ryan climbed out of the car, and James had to take a second to breathe and process that. Ryan didn't seem terribly demonstrative, like most men James knew. The fact that he'd chosen to tell him that right now meant more than James could say. It was kind of the *I love you, man* of a sober guy.

James swallowed hard again to keep himself from getting too emotional and making Ryan uncomfortable. He climbed out of the car and smiled instead, shaking the cash box. "You unload the car, I'll start counting?"

He could use a second to collect his emotions.

"Deal," Ryan smiled, and he tossed James his keys. He only

grinned a little when James totally missed catching them and had to pick them off the ground.

"Shut up," James laughed, shouldering Ryan on the way by, and Ryan even pretended to stumble.

God, Ryan was the sweetest guy James knew.

CHAPTER

Twenty

RYAN

"The sale went really well. Yeah, I'm unloading the car now." Ryan propped the phone between his ear and his shoulder as he pulled open the car door.

"Awesome! Dude, you're Skyping me in tonight, right?"

"Of course," Ryan snorted at Kevin. "Dumbass question. Matty, you there?"

"Yep!" he heard Matty call out in the background. Ryan was on speakerphone with the pair of them. Matty was one of Cam's best friends, and Kevin was a good friend of Ryan's. Somehow, the two hockey players had wound up dating.

"Good. We'll just keep it casual. He'll never suspect a thing." Ryan only had two bins of leftover products to move inside, thanks to how well they'd done.

"He's oblivious enough," Matty laughed. They were sharing a hotel room; he could hear the TV in the background.

"And how's your partner to work with?" Kevin asked. He sounded like he was grinning. "Still distracting you?"

Ryan rolled his eyes. "He's great. Perfect with people. I was just his… wingman," he laughed. "It works great."

"That's a lot of *greats* in there," Kevin snorted. "We'll get to meet him?"

"If Skype counts as meeting, yeah," Ryan laughed, setting down the last bin. Just one more tub of table supplies and then he had to meet James inside. "I gotta go. We're counting up the money."

"Oooh. Awesome. Okay, in an hour, you said?"

"Yep! Maybe two. I'll ask Noah."

"Talk to you in a bit!" Kevin told Ryan.

"Bye!" Matty added in the background.

"See ya." Ryan chuckled and hung up, pocketing his phone again. His friends were dicks sometimes, but he could tell they all—from the Rileys to Floyd and Greyson and Kevin and Matty—genuinely wanted to meet James. He just hoped they didn't scare him off.

He pushed open the front door, then caught his breath.

James was in the middle of his living room floor, money divided into three sets of piles in front of him. He lay on his back, staring up at the ceiling.

James stirred when he opened the door and pushed himself up on his elbows, grinning at Ryan. "Finally."

"Dude, I thought you had a heart attack or something!" Ryan's heart still thumped as he glared at James. He kicked off his shoes to join him in the living room.

James looked startled, then smiled. "Sorry! No, just daydreaming."

"What you'll buy with your money?" Ryan teased without thinking. Then, he winced.

James chuckled at him. "Rent, food, power bill, and then the rest on the credit card."

"Good man," Ryan smiled. He sank next to James and punched his arm. "So tell me!"

"Another four hundred each."

"On top of the six hundred each yesterday?"

James nodded, and for the first time, Ryan noticed that his eyes were a little red.

Christ. He'd been living on a financial edge. Every time they went out, Ryan automatically paid for lunch or supper. That probably made a difference to him. Ryan just hoped he could help him get stable for long enough to get his feet under him properly.

Ryan didn't think twice about hauling him in for a quick, tight hug. That thinner body nestled into his side easily. He didn't realize how tight his hold was until some bone in James's back cracked. "Oops. Sorry."

James was laughing breathily, his arms tightly wrapped around Ryan's waist as he knelt next to him. His weight was supported easily by Ryan's shoulder. "No. It's fine," he murmured, leaning into Ryan's side. "I like being hugged like this."

Ryan's chest warmed at the rough voice near his ear and the scrape of stubble against his jaw. He pressed his face into James's hair for a moment, breathing in his scent. Coconut shampoo and the faint smell of wood polish. James smelled like his workshop now, and that was sexy as hell.

He closed his eyes when James's hand rubbed idle circles along his back. They knelt there, quietly, side by side, James's face pressed into his shoulder.

Ryan finally loosened his hold on James and beamed at him as James straightened up again. Both of them sprawled across the ground, looking at the piles of money. "This is great. Especially for you."

"I can't count on it keeping up, but… if we do as well as I projected from now on? I could pay off my credit card by Christmas."

Ryan's chest warmed as he pulled James in for one more quick, tight hug. "Good for you, man."

The look of gratitude on James's face made Ryan uncomfortable. After all, it was half—or more than half—James's work that had already gotten him this far. Ryan was positive he could have applied those same management skills to anyone's business to get it off the ground.

He was just glad James had chosen him. *His.*

Ryan cleared his throat. "We should head to the barbecue," he suggested, gathering up his pile of money as James took his own. The third went back in the cash box to be deposited to their business bank account.

"Thanks for trusting me," James said, so quietly Ryan almost missed it, as they tugged their shoes on.

Ryan gave him a startled look. "What?"

"With your business. With the money, counting it myself. Everything, I guess," James explained.

God, Ryan wanted to hug him until all those worries melted away, but he resisted the urge. He just smiled for a second, then opened the door and held it for him. "I hear a veggie burger with your name on it."

As they walked to his car, side by side, Ryan realized he'd never felt so excited for a Sunday barbecue, and not just because of what he knew was coming.

He couldn't wait for his friends to meet James. Over years of knowing them, he'd never met a guy he'd wanted to introduce to them.

But James… is different.

CHAPTER
Twenty~One

JAMES

"HE SASSED THOSE ASSHOLES INTO NEXT WEEK."

James's cheeks were hot as he laughed, his hand wrapped tightly around the neck of a beer bottle. Ryan was beaming at him.

He'd been warned the whole crowd would be there, but it was more overwhelming now, in the middle of them.

Cam and Jackson, both of whom he vaguely knew, were the size of Ryan. All three of them jostled each other a lot. Floyd and Greyson, too, were both ripped like they worked out every day. Alex seemed guarded in the presence of someone new, while Thomas watched and listened more. Of all of them, Noah and Chase had welcomed James in with open arms quite literally, hugging him hello.

They hadn't made a big deal about putting on veggie burgers and extra vegetables for him. When he'd tried to thank them, Jackson had waved it off and said they all ought to eat healthier, too.

James was slowly relaxing, even if he didn't quite know how to handle them all, especially at once. "I didn't like them," he said as Ryan recounted the story of him talking to Roger. "They were giving me *that* look."

Noah winced and clapped his back on the way back. "I know the one." He was probably the most fem of all of them, his lisp pronounced and wrist limp. Camp was an understatement. James loved him already.

Better yet, Ryan didn't seem to have a problem with Noah, either, which didn't surprise James by now. Ryan seemed laid-back and willing to take all his friends as they were.

"He's not usually that much of a dick to me," Ryan frowned, looking disappointed for a moment. "And he knows about me."

"That you're gay as the day is bright?" Noah winked. "Why, do you bring your *Playgirl* to work?"

Jackson snorted with laughter.

"No, but… I guess I haven't talked about it, either." Ryan looked sheepish now, glancing over at James. "He didn't seem like he'd be *that* bad."

"It's different for us," Noah said firmly. James shot him a look of appreciation and Noah smiled back at him.

"Yeah," Chase muttered. He was about James's size, even if his rolled-up sleeves showed layers of intricate tattoos. "We've been over this."

Jackson scoffed. "And you guys won't let us go harass them a little."

"Definitely not," James laughed. "It's not that bad. It was just a look. I've had worse."

There was a moment of silence, and James kind of wanted to melt into the floor and take back what he'd just said. Then Ryan touched his back idly, and Jackson jerked his chin at the door. "Someone get the door for me?"

The moment passed, and James let out his breath, heading for the door and pulling it open.

It was a warm, late afternoon for late September. James didn't mind padding out barefoot onto the porch and closing the door behind Jackson. "You need a plate?"

"Yes, please."

He held the plate steady as Jackson moved the veggies and veggie burger onto one plate. He looked away while Jackson got the meat.

"Sorry," Jackson laughed. "Man, I'm glad you guys did well, though."

"Me too." James looked back at Jackson with an appreciative smile. Ryan hadn't told them about his debt, he knew that much. Even so, they'd all applauded Ryan when—with James's permission—he announced their sales total.

"And I'm glad you're around. Ryan's a lot cheerier these days," Jackson smiled.

James tilted his head curiously, handing off the plate to Jackson when he reached for it. He picked up the veggie plate. "Yeah?"

"Yep," Jackson said simply, and offered him another smile. He could sense that Jackson didn't know him well enough to elaborate, but he was trying to welcome him.

It was kind of like being welcomed into their extended circle of family by virtue of dating Ryan. He tried not to think too hard about what that would be like.

If only.

They settled down to eat first, bantering about the show and suggesting products. James had to put down his fork from laughter.

"Oh yeah! Dick-in-a-box boxes," Noah nodded seriously, winking at James. "Pre-wrapped."

Cam had his head tilted back as he laughed. "Noah!" he scolded, elbowing his boyfriend.

"Has *nobody* suggested wooden dildos yet?" Greyson piped up. The ex-cop was grinning at the rest of them. Floyd, his boyfriend, blushed. "Come on."

"I think there's different licensing for that," Thomas hummed. "Health and safety, surely."

"Not if you sell them as *suggested* use, ornamental product." Alex winked. "For external use only."

"Oh my God, you guys," Ryan groaned. He hadn't made eye contact with James since the suggestions began, and James loved it. They were obviously trying to embarrass him and see what happened.

If he didn't want them to know they were kinda-sorta-involved, James could hold his own under pressure. But Ryan? For the strong, silent type, he was blushing a lot.

"Fine, we'll stop," Noah told them, waving the others to hush while he grinned. "So, James, you're not scared off yet?"

James laughed. "Not yet," he told them honestly. It was kind of nice to be around this many guys and have none of them be a dick to him. He wasn't sure if they knew about him yet, which made his stomach jolt with nerves. He could hold off on telling them for now and enjoy it.

"Good. Ryan needs someone to keep him motivated."

"I've noticed," James answered, winking at his business partner.

"I admit it!" Ryan exclaimed, raising his hands. "I work better under external pressure."

James couldn't tell who murmured, "You *wish* he'd externally pressure you," but he laughed as loud as the rest of them at it. Now he was blushing, too, trying not to look at Ryan's bright red cheeks.

"Come on," Cam laughed, pushing himself to his feet. "I'm going to check out that hive. I was told people wanted to see. And Kevin and Matty are online?"

"Oh, yeah!" Ryan winked at James and stood up, going with the distraction. On the way out the door, he waited until the rest of them were outside, then murmured into James's ear, "Sorry."

"No, it's fine," James murmured back. He didn't know how to say *it's nice to be thought of as a catch* without sounding like he was asking for compliments. "I know what it's like being the single friend."

"Oh, Jesus. Tell me about it," Ryan groaned, leading him through the door now. Cam headed down to the bottom of the yard, where the bee hives stood near the back fence. "Okay, Matty and Kevin are online. They'll keep us company."

"They could've come out when I was inspecting this summer," Cam grumbled. "Who's going to bring them around?"

"I'll carry them around," Jackson offered, laughing. "Where's the phone?"

James settled down to sit on the edge of the porch, smiling as Chase came to sit next to him. The other guys were arguing over who got bee suits and who didn't.

"You all right?" Chase asked simply, and James smiled back at him.

"Yeah. I'm good," James answered.

Chase smiled. "Good." Then, he winked and leaned in to whisper, "Big moment coming up."

It didn't take long for James to put two and two together. He caught his breath and stared at Chase. "Is this…?"

"Yep," Chase beamed. It made sense now why he had his

phone out and facing the bee hive, ready to record the moment.

Even though he barely knew any of them, James's heart was light. "Awesome," he murmured, and he meant it.

He hoped he could find the kind of happiness all of these couples seemed to have found in each other. And as his eyes trailed to Ryan, crouching near the hive with a smoking metal device in his hands, James's smile widened.

Maybe… just maybe, it wasn't the *worst* idea to go with what his heart told him.

CHAPTER
Twenty-Two

CAM

Though James had looked skeptical, Cam had managed to encourage him forward for a look at the hive, too. There were only a few in the yard, and he'd already checked the others, apparently. He'd left this one for when his friends were around.

Everyone looked fascinated. Cam had long ago learned that was a universal reaction to bees these days. People wanted to know about the bees dying off, and they wanted to get to know how they lived.

"They won't sting unless you get up in their face," Cam reassured James. "We're just going to check on them, make sure everything looks normal, and seal it up again."

"Cool," James nodded. He looked nervous, but Cam smiled to himself. That would change once he saw inside the hive.

Nobody else had a full bee suit except Cam. He trusted his bees by now not to get too defensive. They were quite used to people walking and playing around their hive, and the queen in there was gentle, which made the bees' temperament gentle, too.

Still, he ushered them all back and puffed smoke in the entrance. Then, he lifted the top cover off and slid his hive tool around the top board to crack it open.

Immediately, fuzzy bee faces peeked up at him. Some bees waved their front legs at him as they stared up at the intruder.

"Hey, girls," he greeted softly, puffing more smoke across the hive until they turned around to head back down into the hive.

"So, this is a..." Cam trailed off, looking into the hive. Something was different: what looked like a box slid into the gap where he'd left a frame out.

Noah's uncle, his boss, was playing tricks on him or something. He eyed the others suspiciously, but everyone just looked clueless.

"Hold on. I think Bill left a gift for me," he laughed. Bill had mentioned a different kind of feeder this year, but this wasn't that at all.

It was a small wooden box with an engraving of a bee on it, and the bees had sealed it shut.

He had to laugh. "Okay, impromptu lesson. They love sealing shit up. See here? They've used propolis, which is a mix of stuff—lots of tree sap—to seal it up, since they couldn't get inside."

Noah laughed from nearby and approached, holding out a hand. Cam shook a few bees off the box, then handed it over to his boyfriend. He lifted out a few frames and checked them.

Everything looked normal—no sign of foul brood or irregular laying patterns, the honey frames were loaded full of honey, and it looked like most of the winter bees had already hatched.

Cam explained what he was doing as he checked the frames. One by one, they approached for a look.

Jackson even brought Kevin and Matty over. They thought the whole thing was even cooler by video where they couldn't get stung.

When Cam slid the frames back into place, he laughed as Noah headed back up the lawn to join the others. Some bees were frantically arriving home to see what had happened while they were away.

"Come on, girls," he coaxed them, sweet-talking them. Cam brushed them gently away from the spots where they could get crushed, then reassembled the hive.

"Now, what the hell did Bill leave me?" Cam laughed. "He knows I have a phone, right?"

It seemed kinda weird to do this, unless he was trying to fill the empty frame space. That way the bees couldn't build crazy comb in there, which was a pain to clean up.

Once the top cover to the hive was on again and the last bees were crawling off him to fly back into their house, Cam unzipped his hood. He stepped out of his suit, then grabbed his hive tool and joined the rest of his friends.

The others were crowding close for a look. Cam took the box from Noah's hands as Noah giggled at the tight seal the bees had made. Gently, Cam slid the metal tool along the cracks in the box lid until it popped slightly, then flipped the latch.

It took him a second to understand what he was seeing. In that time, Noah gently took the box from his hands and was kneeling in the grass in front of him again.

A few bees still buzzed nearby, crawling over Cam's back

and Noah's shoulder. Cam had nearly forgotten them. In the middle of the box, a wide gold band was neatly peeking out from the gap in a velvet cushion.

Holy. Fucking. Shit. This isn't...?

"Cameron Riley," Noah murmured, his voice already choked up.

Instinctively, Cam's chest felt tight, and he cleared his throat quietly. *It is.*

"The gentlest, sweetest man I know with his girls, and with all his friends, and especially with me," Noah murmured, his eyes wet. "The second I saw you, I knew I wanted you."

Someone cat-called in the background, and both Cam and Noah laughed.

"Every day, I'm so glad you came to my table," Noah murmured. "You walked into my life, and... it was never the same. Everything we've done, and built together?" He gestured at their little friendship group, and the group of houses behind them. "Everything we went through, last year?" *My heart. The diagnosis... at last. The surgery.* Cam didn't interrupt, but he nodded to show he knew what he meant. "Christ, Cam, I wouldn't trade it for *anything.*"

Cam wanted to sink to his knees and hug Noah. He resisted the urge yet, letting his sweet, sweet boyfriend say his piece before he started crying.

Too late, because Noah's cheeks were wet now, too, as he laughed sheepishly. Those beautiful, wide eyes gazed up at Cam as he clutched the ring box.

"Cam, before I'm a sobbing mess, I'll just... ask... will you marry me?"

"*Yes,*" Cameron breathed out. His hands shook as he held the left one out. Noah's delicate fingers slid the ring on like he was a work of art Noah was carefully installing in his gallery.

Then, Cam grabbed Noah's upper arms to haul him up to his feet and kissed the *hell* out of him.

It took him a few seconds to remember that anyone else was around, let alone to tune into the cheers and realize they were for *them*.

His eyes burned as he pressed his face into Noah's shoulder for a few more seconds. Then, he pulled himself together as they hugged so tightly he felt Noah's breath rush out of him.

Cam had half-expected Noah to be the one to propose, but never for it to be in such a mischievous, mysterious way. "You sneaky bastard," Cam laughed, finally pulling back for another slow kiss.

Noah was on tip-toe, his arms loosely draped around Cam's neck. His wrist was bent and head cocked, his hip out at an angle as he beamed back at him. "I'm glad I can still surprise you."

"Holy shit," Cam laughed, rubbing his eyes with his wrist for a second before looking at his friends and brothers. Then they were there, hugging him—Thomas and Jackson first, and then his other friends, so close they might as well be brothers.

Even James, the newest to the circle, clapped his back in congratulations while Ryan hugged him. And Cam, despite his joy, didn't miss the look that was exchanged between them.

They so want each other. But Cam didn't tease them yet—he was patient. He'd wait and see to be proven right.

For now, Cam couldn't stop smiling. Noah had his arm wrapped around his, giggling at every single thing people said, absolutely high off life. For at least the ten-thousandth time, he knew he'd made the right damn choice in choosing *this* man.

"Did you get Bill's help?"

"Nope, I put it there myself," Noah bragged, beaming away. "Last night when you and Jackson went out to the bar to watch the game."

"Holy shit, in the dark? And you didn't get stung?"

"I'm the bee whisperer," Noah bragged, leaning into Cam as he wrapped his arm tightly around his fiancé's shoulder.

"I never doubted that," Cam said warmly, waiting for Noah to look at him. He kissed those beautiful lips again and ran his hand back through Noah's blond, undercut, soft hair.

Then, Cam spotted Chase holding his phone sideways and grinning.

"Are you recording me? Oh, shit, nobody needs to see that," Cam laughed, swatting at the camera as Chase tried to hold it out of his reach.

But if a few of them had teary eyes, it was for all the right reasons.

As Jackson came back with a case of beer and Thomas brought out a cake, it occurred to Cam that he might have been the only one not to know what was about to go on. For a bunch of ten-year-olds at heart, they'd all kept Noah's secret for—God knew how long.

Just so Cam could be completely surprised.

Cam's cheeks hurt from smiling as he reached out with his beer bottle, clinking it against everyone else's. "Thanks, guys."

There was so much layered in that thank you that he couldn't say: *thanks for living here, thanks for being there for me, thanks for joining my family.*

As James leaned into Ryan and Ryan wrapped an arm absentmindedly around James's waist like he didn't even know he was doing it, Cam suspected their little family was about to grow.

Still so conscious of the warm metal ring on his finger, Cam ran a hand down Noah's arm as the hubbub of excited voices rose and fell around them.

"We're going to get you a matching ring this week," Cam murmured to Noah.

Noah tangled their fingers, leaning into him and pressing his lips into Cam's neck. "I can't wait." Then, he giggled in a bare whisper, "Think we should start keeping an eye out for Ryan's?"

Cam chuckled back and nodded at his new fiancé, glad he wasn't the only one to have noticed.

Despite the dying summer, the crisp autumn air was full of love, and it was about damn time.

CHAPTER
Twenty~Three

RYAN

RYAN WASN'T SQUEAKING WITH EXCITEMENT LIKE CHASE OR slapping Cam's back like Jackson. Still, he couldn't stop smiling as he drove James home.

"That was sickeningly sweet," James laughed, rolling his head against the back of the seat. A smile played on his lips. He was glowing, and Ryan could tell he was just as happy despite barely knowing them.

"Wasn't it?" Ryan chuckled deeply. "Of all my friends, they've been together the longest. I knew it was coming—not just because I did the box, but just because they're so... you know, *right.*"

"Yeah," James nodded. "Sometimes you look at a couple and you just see their chemistry."

There was a moment of silence. When Ryan's gaze flickered across to James, he caught James looking at him. Like he was a third-grader, heat rose to Ryan's cheeks.

Oh, for God's sake. Just get it out.

"Strictly-business is hard around you," Ryan stated. He kept his grip firm on the wheel as he let the other hand rest on the gearshift. That whole barbecue, staying by James's side and keeping his touches to a back-clap every once in a while? Tortuous.

James let out a breathy laugh. "Yeah, I'm glad you mentioned that."

"I've thought about you a lot," Ryan admitted, keeping his words as simple and plain as usual. He didn't see the point in dancing around the point. "I know it's not practical, but… I don't often get stuck on someone."

"Me neither," James said, and then that smaller hand pressed over his on the gearshift. A shiver of pleasure coursed through Ryan as his grip tightened. He cast another quick smile at the guy in his passenger seat.

Or maybe the driver's seat. He wasn't sure which of them was steering this, but he suspected it was James, if anyone.

"That's why we have the legal stuff drawn up," James said. His thumb rubbed slow circles against Ryan's knuckles. "In case anything went south. I don't think you're the type of guy to get vindictive anyway, right? Neither am I. We could figure something out."

Ryan let out a quick breath of relief. "Yeah. I was worried 'cause you have more to lose."

James looked thoughtful for a moment before his lips curved up in a quick smile. "The fact that you thought of that means a lot, honestly. But I'm willing to take a risk for…"

For me? Ryan's heart jolted with surprise. He didn't want to be presumptuous and fill in the word, but it seemed like that was where the sentence was going.

He cast another quick glance at James.

James's cheeks were red as he offered a little grin. "For whatever this could be."

Yeah. Taking it slow, Ryan reminded himself. They'd made

out once. That wasn't the basis of a solid relationship… yet. Still, there was an itch inside that told him he knew enough about James already.

They would be *so* good together.

Ryan pulled up to James's house. He barely had the parking brake engaged before James's hand ran up from his hand along arm, then rested on his shoulder.

"Come in."

Ryan didn't have to think twice about that. He unbuckled and leaned over the gap between them to grab a quick kiss. James smiled, his eyes sliding shut as his hand rose to tangle in the hair at the back of Ryan's neck. Before they got too caught up in the moment, Ryan pulled back again with a quick smile, then slid out of his side of the car.

"Mm." James almost wriggled out of his seat. He strutted up the sidewalk beside Ryan toward the back building where his apartment was located. Though they didn't hold hands, they stood too close, the heat building between them.

James was a crystal in front of the sun, amplifying the heat and desire Ryan felt for him. Hell, he was the whole fucking sun.

Ryan barely lasted until they were inside James's front door before he grabbed James's shoulders. He pulled him in for a kiss that was hard and heartfelt.

James rose onto tiptoe, his arms sliding around Ryan's neck as his lithe body pressed against Ryan's. His knee rose, sliding up Ryan's outer thigh like he wanted to hang onto him.

Their lips pressed hotly together, warm mouths and tongues and sparks flying. Their teeth clicked once, but then Ryan figured out the trick to kissing him despite the height difference and tilted his head just right.

"Mm, you're *good*," James breathed out against Ryan's lips. Damn, if that didn't make him want to prove it in other ways.

Ryan gave James a quick, breathless grin as he pressed a few more kisses along the cute young guy's jaw. "Should we sit down, at least?"

James moaned in mock protest and let go of Ryan, sidling out of his hold in a quick swish of his hips and sauntering over to the couch. "If you insist." Then, he said something else, but Ryan's brain didn't click into place quite in time. He was busy enjoying the view.

"Huh?" Ryan grinned.

James's grin only widened as he flopped on the couch and patted the spot next to him. "C'mere, cheeky."

Ryan was only too glad to collapse on the couch. "I guess I don't have to ask if we're gonna do anything."

"Oh, I hope so," James told him, smirking. "I haven't been carrying condoms to your place for nothing."

Ryan was positive his face was crimson. That meant James had been thinking of—at least—blowjobs, or some kind of sex. Ahead of time. Thinking of sex, with him, ahead of time. James was laughing at him, which confirmed his suspicions. He rubbed his ear and nodded. "God, I like that you speak your mind."

"Couldn't stop me," James promised, shifting on the couch until he straddled Ryan. The warm pressure of his thighs—and bulge—pressing against Ryan's was addictive.

"Good." Ryan ran his hand up James's back to pull him close. Their stomachs and chests met by the time his hand reached the back of James's neck and his lips pressed hard against James's.

James had to know how grinding against his lap was

going to affect him, right? Ryan gasped against James's lips. The way he moved his hips in slow, deliberate circles and the gleam in James's eyes told Ryan that yeah, he knew.

"You're easy to fluster," James pointed out with a cheeky smile.

Ryan was throbbing with desire, his nails digging into James's back. "When you look at me like *that*, I am."

James pulled back to look Ryan up and down, his hand running up under Ryan's shirt. The slender palm pressed firmly against his bare skin, teasing the skin from his stomach to his chest, then tweaking his nipple. "Like what?"

Ryan's laugh escaped in a quick rush of breath. He grabbed James's cheeks, palms scraping on stubble, to pull him in and kiss those smiling lips.

James was just *fun* to be around. Every time he thought that, or something similar, it felt like all the pieces were there in front of him. He just wasn't sure how to put them together and win James over to the idea. Or did he even have to win James over? James seemed pretty damn into this, too.

Ryan raised his arms to let James pull his t-shirt off. He fought the material away and leaned back against the couch as James lowered his lips to his collarbone. The grazes of lips and sucking warmth against his sensitive skin sent white-hot prickles of need through him. It was all he could do not to grab James's hips and grind up against him.

James was actually trying to drive him crazy.

As if he read his mind, James ran his hand down to the bulge at Ryan's groin and rubbed in slow circles with his palm.

Oh, Christ, that felt good.

James leaned in to lip Ryan's ear and Ryan shoved his hips

up into James's palm, his eyes sliding closed. He craved relief, but he could hold on a little more.

"There are way too many clothes going on." James leaned back, his ass firmly against Ryan's knees. His fingers glided down the row of buttons along his chest, popping each open in turn until he shrugged his shirt off. He leaned back and tossed it aside with a grin.

James was thin but strong. Ryan's eyes skated for a moment along the red, raised scars under his pecs. He had a treasure trail leading up from his jeans to his belly button. Ryan couldn't resist running his finger along the coarse hair.

"Oof," James squirmed with a laugh.

"Good?"

"Oh yeah, I don't mind," James smirked as Ryan's hand continued up through the light fuzz on his chest. When Ryan hesitated over his ribs, James covered Ryan's hand to push it further up to his nipples. "It was two years ago now. It's impossible to tell if the sensation's the *same* as before. Either way, the scar tissue gives me extra—different—sensation. The scars themselves are okay to touch."

"Right." Ryan hadn't known how to ask, but he carefully memorized that information. He pulled James in by his sides, admiring the core strength he could feel running through his torso and up his back. Those strong arms came from James hauling himself up cliff faces. He lipped at James's chest, bending his neck so his lips reached James's nipples.

"Aw, *fuck.*" James was grinding into him, his breathing suddenly shallow as he rocked his hips.

Ryan smirked, pressing open-mouthed kisses around the pink nub. He closed in on it and flicked the tip of his tongue across a few times.

The rough, loud gasp that escaped James told him to try that a few more times. He did, and sucked on it the last time.

"Ry-Ryan, holy hell."

Ryan's eyes crinkled with pleasure at James's breathy moan. He wanted to earn that reaction more from James. He ran his hand slowly up James's back all the way to the back of his neck. He let his fingertip trail to his earlobe and up to his jaw, then grabbed his chin for a quick, firm kiss of their lips together. Then, he returned his attention to James's other nipple.

James was groaning now, his grip on Ryan's shoulders tightening. He kneaded his fingers into the muscles near Ryan's biceps. His lips were parted, his head rolled back to expose his throat as he gulped and his Adam's apple bobbed. Ryan couldn't resist kissing it on his way up James's neck to his lips.

"Your mouth's fuckin' dirty," James accused him with a breathless grin against his lips. He sucked Ryan's lip between his before Ryan could answer.

Ryan growled under his breath with agreement. His body jolted with heat once more at James's tongue flicking along the sensitive skin of his lip.

The second James let his lip go, their lips mashed hard as they pushed into each other, tongues seeking tongues. Warm hands cupped each other's cheeks as their groins ground together, hardness into hardness.

Ryan was half-dizzy by the time James pulled back for breath and to whisper, "What do you like doing?"

"Anything you wanna do," Ryan admitted, running his thumb along James's rib. He tried to resist bringing James's mind back to his scar, even if his human impulse was to trace it. "I... really want you."

The words didn't seem adequate to convey the lust that pounded through his solid frame. Even James's light weight against his made him want to thrust up into it—or down into it, perhaps. Oh, fuck, that sounded good.

James smirked slowly, those lips so fucking divine that they distracted Ryan from his words for a split-second. Then, he scooted backward off Ryan's lap and onto the floor between Ryan's knees. He pushed them apart and grabbed Ryan by the thighs to haul him closer to the edge of the couch.

"Oh, fuck, yes." Ryan was bursting to be freed from the denim prison of his jeans, and the prospect of that hot mouth on him? He moaned when James's hand slowly ran over the hard outline of his cock, then slid his zipper down.

That sound sent a thrill through him.

He raised his hips to help James slide his pants down. His hard cock ached with momentary relief, then need once more.

Best of all was the look in James's eye—mischievous and in control, yet hungry for him. He ran a hand over his own cheeks, licking his palm and rubbing his thumb along his lower lip as he gazed at the hardened length. He reached out to wrap his warm, wet hand around the shaft and slid his tight grip to the base of it for a stroke or two.

Ryan couldn't have pictured a hotter sight or feeling. The tight ring around him felt so perfect that all he managed was a quick grunt of approval. Sense swam to him from some corner of his mind, and he patted the couch for his jeans.

"I got one."

That made Ryan grin. "Right. The one you've been saving for me," he teased. James laughed, flicking his thigh in a quick scolding for his cheek.

Had he been saving it for him? The thought was hot enough to keep him thoroughly distracted until the tight ring of fingers slid down his shaft. It was followed instantly by a hot mouth.

"Oh, *fuck!*"

He almost had to check if the condom was on properly, it felt so fucking raw, but it was. Good brand. He had to ask later—

James's cheeks sucked in around his shaft. That was it for rational thought. The heat and pressure alone were enough to jolt Ryan along from his frustrated suspense into pleasure that rocked through his whole body.

His muscles tightened and he tensed against the couch with a sharp exhalation. "*God.* Yes."

James kept his fingers tight around his cock as he slid his hand back up along with his mouth. He bobbed his head in long, slow sucks of his mouth to take him in to the back of his throat.

"How'd you get so fucking *good*? Jesus!" Ryan wasn't complaining one bit. As James's fingers gently caressed his balls and came up the underside of his shaft, it sent another electric jolt through him until his toes curled into the floor. He needed *something* to say to distract him from coming in three more seconds.

Mercifully, James popped his mouth off his cock and chuckled. He started kissing along his erection from top to bottom as he murmured, "A little intuition, a little magic..."

"I bet you have a five-sta—wait, do guys leave reviews on Grindr?"

For a second, James stared at him like he wasn't sure he was serious, which answered Ryan's question. Then he threw his head back and burst out laughing, his rich voice echoing off the walls as his teeth flashed in a broad grin.

Ryan's cheeks flushed as he mumbled, "Okay, now that I know not, that sounds like an insult. Can I take that back?"

"Absolutely not," James managed. He tongued the spot where the head met the shaft until Ryan's head rolled back into the back of the couch and he was distracted from his mortification. "I'm making sure you never forget that."

"Jesus," Ryan mumbled, only half from embarrassment. James was sucking him back between his lips, his lips tight around the throbbing length. Ryan's muscles twitched and his chest tightened. "Oh, fuck, James—fuck, that's... oh, Jesus."

He hadn't had anyone blow him in too many fuckin' months. He was going to come any moment now, but he wanted his eyes open. Needed to see those dark eyes hungrily eye his dick as it disappeared between those sinful pink lips, and scan his face for approval and arousal.

Ryan was utterly safe in James's hands. It was a weird thought to have out of the blue, but James's thumb gently rubbed his inner thigh in a move that was more affectionate than sensual. He caught the expression of genuine pleasure crossing James's face when he groaned. Maybe that thought wasn't so out of the blue.

It wasn't just the chemistry making his body sizzle; his muscles twitched and tightened involuntarily at the warmth and pressure. James bobbed his head faster, his tongue caressing the underside of his shaft every time it disappeared between his lips.

And then Ryan came, utterly forgetting everything else around except James. James's hot mouth pursed around him.

His beautiful brown eyes gazed up Ryan's body to drink in every look on his face. His hand crept up from his thigh to play with his nipple until Ryan's body shuddered with over-sensitivity and he gasped for mercy.

Ryan slumped back into the couch with another moan as James pulled his lips off his softening shaft and peeled off the condom. "Fucking *hell*," he told James.

"I'll take that. That'll be the title of your five-star review, huh?" James gave a cheeky grin as he stood up, presumably to dump the condom in a trash can.

The second he returned, Ryan grabbed James, ignoring his laughter and kissing him as he pulled him down onto his lap. He almost had to wrestle him onto there, especially when he smacked James's ass. "Cheeky."

"You like me that way," James retorted, squirming against his thigh with a quiet moan. "But if you're gonna do *that*, you'd better follow through." He pressed another long, warm kiss against Ryan's lips, then kissed along his neck and shoulder. Ryan's cock softened and clearheaded sense swam back to him.

Ryan caught his breath and pressed a kiss behind James's ear. "What do you like?"

"It depends what guys feel comfortable with."

Ryan pulled back to get a look at James's face. "In a perfect world?"

"I love blowjobs, too," James admitted with a grin. "Sometimes I let them get off with hand jobs or whatever. Sometimes I'll get myself off. It depends."

"I want to suck you off, too," Ryan murmured, running his hands down James's sides with a warm smile. "Scoot over."

James grinned and Ryan kissed him as they rolled together, then laughed. "What—where are you? Oh."

"Hi." James was lying sideways along the couch now, his head on the armrest. He grabbed Ryan by the shoulders to haul him in for another kiss.

Ryan wished he could just nestle between James's legs and kiss him for, like, another hour, but James would kill him if he teased him *that* much. Instead, he kissed back a few more times, then started to kiss down across James's chest.

A few spots above James's nipples made his whole body shudder and tense up. It was easy to read the reactions in his lean body: almost painful pleasure. Ryan kissed straight down to his waistband, then mouthed at his stomach and hips as he fought James's tight jeans off, leaving him just in his underwear.

"Damn your fashionable choices."

James winked. "You hate me looking good on your arm, I know. I'll dress in potato sacks from now on."

"Good. Easier access."

The way James's cheeks flushed and his hips shifted up to grind into Ryan's hand made Ryan smirk in triumph. He ran his hand along the shaft, aiming to help him grind into it, and he was rewarded by James pushing into his hand a few more times.

"Y-Yeah," James moaned. "To whatever you just said."

Ryan let his voice drip with suggestive teasing. It was easy to be seductive with *this* man squirming for his attention. "Oh, you heard me. You have a condom for you, or what?" He wasn't sure how that worked.

"Yeah," James told him with a laugh. He raised his hips to push his tight underwear down. There was more underwear underneath—black and strappy, holding James's dick in place.

God, that was more realistic than Ryan had expected. The hard shaft lying against James's thigh made him lick his lips as he gazed from it up to James's face. "Can I...?"

"Oh, yeah," James grinned. "Please do."

Ryan ran his hand from the base of the shaft to the tip, squeezing lightly. It felt... damn close to what he'd have expected, actually. Warm, velvety, and hard. When James guided his hand, he bent the shaft up and nodded in understanding.

He'd be lying if he said it didn't get his imagination racing. Did James ever top?

"I can see your brain racing there," James teased, making heat flush through Ryan's cheeks. "Talk to me."

Of course. It wasn't fair to leave him hanging. Ryan grinned. "It's hot," he told James. "Do you ever top, too...?"

"Mmhmm." James was grinning, his body flushed with arousal still. That brought Ryan's focus back to what he wanted to do for him.

"So, I'm guessing you don't want me to suck this cock?"

"Yeah, it looks good, but the one under it feels better," James chuckled. His hand ran down Ryan's cheek to cup it for a moment.

Ryan nodded, stroking that shaft once more before grinding it against James for a moment. It made James's hips arch as his breath caught in his throat. "Like matryoshka. The Russian nesting dolls."

James's laugh was rich and loud again as he went from breathlessly aroused to amused in seconds, his eyes lighting up. There was a newfound appreciation in his eyes as he gazed at Ryan. "Yeah. Something like that."

A little smarter than I play. Ryan winked and brought his thumbs to the straps of James's jockstrap. "So, can I?"

"Long as you fucking hurry up with it," James grinned. He raised his hips to help Ryan ease down the fabric and silicone. Ryan licked his lips at the sight as James settled on the couch again, then tore open the condom packet with his teeth.

James's chest was rising and falling quickly. His body flinched at every little touch of Ryan's palm along his treasure trail to his stomach, then down to his hip. His flushed arousal peeked out from his foreskin.

Ryan was entranced, but not enough not to tease him. He ran his finger slowly up the inside of James's thigh, grinning as James moaned and his whole body arched off the couch. "It's bigger than I expected. Yum."

"*Christ,*" James groaned, trying to keep his breathing under control. He paused in the middle of unrolling the condom to clutch his outer thigh. "Years of T does that. You're..."

"I'm what?" Ryan teased, grinning as he pressed a slow kiss to James's stomach. "Hurry up."

James eyed him and laughed, then ripped the tip off the condom with his teeth. He twisted the bottom rim and tore that off with his teeth.

"Like an animal," Ryan smirked, sliding down the couch until he could press his mouth to the hair on the inside of his thigh.

James only had a wordless groan in response. He nipped a tear in the tube, then ripped it straight down the center and tossed the rectangle at Ryan. "Bastard."

"Nah. I'll follow through." Ryan caught it and winked, sliding it onto James's body with an extra rub of his palm as he kissed his way up James's inner thigh. By the time he reached James's cock, James was writhing with pleasure.

It wasn't hard to figure out what to do. He wrapped his lips around the head and slid his lips down to the base, easily swallowing it through the thin barrier. No gag reflex to worry about, at least. James throbbed with pleasure, his stomach heaving for breath already as Ryan's tongue flicked back and forth across the head.

"God, yes! You know how to suck a guy," James moaned. When Ryan looked up, he saw that James was groaning it into his fist. His other hand rubbed Ryan's shoulder.

Ryan took James's hands and moved them to his hair, then tightened his lips around the shaft. He started slowly pulling his head back and pushing it down again, keeping his tongue moving around the head the whole time.

"R-Ryan, fuck, yes," James panted, his hips pushing up. With Ryan's encouragement, his hands tightened in his hair. James pushed up into his mouth each time his head bobbed down.

All the gorgeous noises spilling from his throat were entrancing. Ryan was burning with heat at James's reactions, half-wishing they'd just hurried up and done this the first time they met.

But it was more than worth the wait, because he could read James's expression now—every wince as he tried to slow himself down, every squeeze of his eyes shut as he tried to get control of himself, and then the slow smile across his lips that meant he was in fucking bliss and he didn't care about that anymore.

"You're so fucking *hot,*" Ryan breathed out hoarsely. He licked around the head slowly as he looked up to look James straight in the eye.

James stared at him open-mouthed like he wanted to memorize this sight.

"Tell me if you want anything else," Ryan murmured, his fingers teasing the inside of James's thigh.

"Just… *this*, some more, but faster." James grinned, the muscles in his hips twitching as he tried not to thrust up in response to Ryan's touches.

Ryan moaned and bobbed his head faster now, keeping his lips firmly pursed around James's dick to tug as he sucked. James's writhing and moaning under him, and the way he thrust and ground up into his mouth… all of it was going to be stuck in his head for *weeks* now.

James threw his head back as he groaned. "Ryan, I'm almost—oh my God, yes!" He throbbed in Ryan's mouth, his whole body shivering and clenching. He let go of Ryan's hair and grabbed the edge of the couch instead, pressing his heels into the couch. He was pushing up with quick, sharp thrusts of pleasure. "Yes! Oh, fuck, fuck, fuck…" James's breathy groan scratched its way from his throat, his stomach heaving for breath.

Ryan tried to judge the pace and slowed his movements, letting go of the suction. Finally, he pulled his head up off James and licked his lips. Holy shit, that was *hot*.

James had his eyes closed and his arm over his eyes, but his cheeks were bright red, his chest flushed with arousal and breath still fast.

"You're fuckin' gorgeous," Ryan informed him in an undertone, running his hand carefully up James's thigh and side to his chest.

When James opened his eyes, still looking hazy, he grinned and grabbed Ryan by the shoulder. "C'mere."

Ryan let James pull him up, squeeze his knees around his

waist, and kiss him hard. "Mmm," he moaned back, tongues sliding against tongues and warm lips caressing lips. Best of all, the way James's arm lazily wrapped around his back, James's thin body pressed under his…

Ryan's body still throbbed with pleasure of his own, but more than that, his chest ached with… happiness.

He hadn't had a hookup in years, if ever, that left him feeling this good. It couldn't just be the hormones, right?

When he pulled back from the kiss at last, he braced himself with an arm over James's head. James was lazily smiling back at him in a way that told him it wasn't just him.

Fuck. This was serious.

Ryan shifted to ease himself up, still smiling at James and rubbing his face. "Jesus. Wow."

"You gonna take off on me?" James grinned, pushing himself up to sit up on the couch. He grabbed his own condom to throw away. "You the love-him-and-leave-him type?"

"No, I have to stop by the yard before it closes and grab those pine boards. I like that I made you come so hard you forgot all about my schedule," Ryan winked as he dressed.

"Oh, shit, yeah," James laughed. He leaned against his kitchen counter to drink a glass of water. He shifted it to the other hand and smacked Ryan's ass when he passed by on the way to the bathroom. "Now who's cheeky?"

"I can be," Ryan agreed, cracking his jaw and licking his lips with a suggestive wink.

James bit his lip, those gorgeous dark eyes falling to the floor for just a second of flirting before he waved his hand. "Go on, get cleaned up before I keep you here and you lose out on our deal."

Ryan's chest was still warm, and he was relaxed, yet purposeful as he strode for the bathroom. He couldn't remember the last time his cheeks hurt so much from smiling.

173

CHAPTER
Twenty~Four

JAMES

"You've done all that in only the last... two months?"

"It sounds like a lot, but it's just a little every day." James waved with the hand not holding his wine glass, but he was glowing with pride. That was his father's way of telling him he was proud of him.

His dad, Luke, was leaning back, looking across the table at Anna. His dad's girlfriend was a few years younger than Luke and had no kids of her own. She never seemed sure how to handle kids, so she treated James like one of his dad's friends. His parents had split up years ago but she'd come into the picture three years ago, so it worked.

They were pretty good to him. If they'd had more room in the house, he'd be glad to stay with them over Thanksgiving. Unfortunately, he was stuck staying at his mom's. After the last craft show on Friday, he'd taken a bus straight here and crashed at his mother's house. Since he didn't have a car, his dad had picked him up for Saturday dinner.

"Good for you, though," Anna spoke up. "You look a lot

healthier and happier than you did when you were job-hunting."

His dad glanced back at him and nodded. "It's true."

"Thanks," James smiled. He felt exactly what they meant: he walked taller these days and looked strangers in the eye more readily. He even occasionally answered the phone without that yawning sense of dread in his stomach. "It's been great for me."

Having a job—not just a job, but a business—as much as he hated to admit it, focused him. It gave him something to *do* that felt good. Their last show had gone almost as well as the two before. They were already lined up for three more as soon as he was back from Thanksgiving. Ryan had been working flat-out on production while James learned more about how to finish them.

They kissed sometimes in passing—James initiating more than Ryan, who still came off as shy sometimes. They hadn't gone further since their night of passion just over a week ago. They were too busy working flat-out to replenish their inventory. Unlike many woodworkers and craft business owners, they hadn't had the summer to stock up.

James welcomed the challenge despite the heart-attack moments—realizing they were out of glue, or they needed a different stain color, or they'd forgotten to rinse out the brushes.

James rose to his feet to take their plates. "Thank you for supper," he told Dad and Anna, bringing everything to the sink to start washing up.

"No, leave that, we'll take care of it," Anna assured him. "You're very welcome. It would be nice to see you more, but I guess you'll be stuck up there, hm?"

"Yeah, it's hard to get away between now and Christmas,"

James nodded. "Craft shows every weekend we can get them. If we had a damn market stall, income would be more reliable. Our schedule would settle down..." he trailed off, then sighed. He wasn't about to drag up whatever the hell was going on with Ryan's coworkers.

"You'll figure out a way to get one," his dad said, and James's annoyance faded.

His dad sounded confident in him.

James had almost forgotten what that sounded like from a parent. He didn't talk to him often enough—his dad stayed busy with his job and building a new cabin, and James was pretty bad at checking in. It was only because Mom bugged him with phone calls and texts that he talked to her more.

"Thanks. Yeah. I will."

Conversation turned to other topics like the neighbors and Anna's coworkers. James found himself disappointed when he got the text from his mom.

Will you be home tonight?

"Knowing your mom, that's a hint," Dad gently laughed. They hadn't exactly split up on great terms. They'd done their best to keep James from being in the middle, though.

James grimaced. "Yeah, I guess so." He rose to his feet.

"I'll give you a ride back," his dad told James, so he nodded his thanks and hugged Anna goodbye.

"Take care of yourself," Anna said warmly, and it made James smile. Her understanding of his situation was pretty basic, but she respected him. That was probably why it felt like she treated him like an adult, not her boyfriend's dumb kid.

"I will, thanks. You, too."

James shivered with the nip of the autumn night air as his

dad led him out to the car. He waved once more to Anna before buckling up.

"Maybe I can come over to your place for Christmas," James suggested tentatively. His mom had only let him do that twice as a teen, but both years had been among the best James could remember.

Dad looked genuinely torn. "I'd love that, kid, but Anna's family wants to see her."

"Oh, you're going over to her family for Christmas? Must be serious," James smiled, glancing at the houses they passed. He couldn't help but feel like he was being led back to the herd for slaughter.

"It is," his dad said.

James looked over quickly. Was he trying to tell him something? "You two going to get engaged or something?" he asked after a moment.

"We've been thinking about it." His dad was better than him at hiding his feelings, like most guys. There was no mistaking the hopeful glow in his voice.

James grinned. "Jesus, everyone's getting engaged lately," he laughed. "Congratulations… in advance, I guess."

His dad laughed. "Thanks. Everyone?"

"A couple guys I know just did," James explained simply.

"Ahh."

His dad was good about the gay thing, too—had been even after the trans thing. That had been kind of a one-two punch. James knew by now that his father's main worry was always for his happiness and safety.

"I think I've met someone, too," James said after a moment. Hell, if he wasn't gonna see his dad for months, he kind of wanted him to know. He didn't know where the hell this was going with Ryan, but…

He wanted it to go *somewhere*.

"Oh? Do I get to meet him?"

"Not yet," James smiled. "It's early days yet. But something feels different. I'd like it to be."

His father reached over to punch his arm gently as he came to a stop by the final light before his mother's house. "I'm glad for you, son. As long as he treats you right." He was out of his depth, but trying his hardest, and it made James relent and grin back at him.

"Of course, Dad." James chuckled. That protectiveness, at least, hadn't changed. "I won't break his heart either."

"Good man," his father approved. He pulled away from the light to round the corner to his mother's street. "Looks like the whole clan's just about left—that's just your mom's car and, what, your aunt's?"

"Yes," James grimaced. Aunt Kay was his least favorite. She liked to "accidentally" deadname him. Worse yet, she was invited to Sunday dinner, even though he'd specifically asked his mom not to ask her.

Family politics.

"You need anything, you can call," his father told him, pulling the parking brake once he was at the bottom of the driveway. He turned to face James. "Good luck with them."

James laughed. "If I don't make it out, remember me."

"Will do."

"Thanks for supper, again, Dad. And I'm really happy for you and Anna." His father smiled back at him as James leaned in to hug him tightly. "Keep me up to date on the engagement."

"You'll be the first to know," his dad promised, clapping his back. "See you soon, James."

"Bye, Dad."

James's heart hurt to walk out of that car, but he was almost tingly from the high of it. An adult, man-to-man conversation with his dad. Dad had always been pretty good, but the timing of it was the best part of tonight. It felt like armor against the battles he knew stood between him and the Thanksgiving tofu turkey.

"Does that have to sit for so long? I didn't think it would help."

James tried not to get impatient with his aunt. Kay hovered in the kitchen, getting in his way while he took the tray of tofu out of the fridge.

"Yeah, the longer you let it marinate, the more flavor it has. Like any other meat." He stirred the marinade around the tofu slices, then flipped them again.

"Any other meat," she repeated with a laugh, and James's irritation prickled again. "So, we're thinking a girls' night in, maybe watch some chick flicks and popcorn?"

James's annoyance must have shown on his face, but it didn't seem to be stopping her. He hadn't even shaved for the last week. He'd let himself grow out from stubble to the beginning of a full beard now. He'd gotten genetically lucky from his dad. He grew plenty of stubble along his jaw and cheeks, under his lip and chin. He looked more his age and less twinky when he had it.

More importantly, the dark, thick beard was a pretty huge clue to obstinate family members. They could fuck off with their "girls' nights in" and their talking about James behind his back.

"Right. I'll head upstairs and leave you to it," James

nodded. He sprinkled more parsley into the marinade to give his hands something to do other than dig his nails into his palm.

Aunt Kay laughed like he'd told a funny joke. "No, silly, you're invited too."

"Oh, sorry. I thought you meant you and Mom. It's been a while since I've been the gay best friend," James said dryly. There was an out for her, at least, if she cared to take it. He'd long ago figured out that one gay guy was allowed in a girls' night in. He just had to ogle men and know something about fashion or makeup.

She ignored him altogether. "I'm thinking whatever comes on TV, but if you want to start up Netflix, you can."

James couldn't think of anything he wanted to do less than sit around with his mom and his aunt and whoever else wound up coming over. Still, he didn't have any better options. He had to try to keep the peace until Thanksgiving supper was over tomorrow.

"Sure. I'll pick something," he said. He slid the tray of tofu back in the fridge and made a break for the armchair before anyone else could claim it.

* * *

It was hard to remember a time when James felt worse. This beat the hell out of lunch dates and suppers with his mom. Even beat that time last summer on his cousin's dock, yelling at each other until they both cried from frustration and anger.

He was curled up into a ball on the armchair, the princess movie droning in the background—one of his favorites. Aunt Kay and his mother were talking over it. His least favorite cousins, Leila and Jo, had joined them. Both of them had been absolute fashion queens growing up, so he'd never had much in common with them. He got the distinct feeling they were laughing at him every time they met.

Leila was around his age, but Jo was younger—she was just in her first year of university now.

"Don't let them sucker you into a credit card," his mom was busy telling Jo. "They'll offer you iPads and iTampons and whatever else—"

"Aunty G!" Jo protested with a mortified laugh. "It's a tablet."

"Whatever else, dear," Mom told her and waved a hand. "But just ask James."

They were *barely* using his name. He knew damn well that every time he left the room, they didn't. It was in the way they stumbled when they said the first syllable, or when they had to use a pronoun.

It was so fucking childish, all of it. It would be a hundred times easier for them to just use one name, one pronoun. One that would make sense to anyone who saw them address the scrawny bearded guy in the living room.

The only reason they didn't was some kind of family politics. They wanted to make him earn it—a game he wasn't playing.

"Ask me what?" he stated flatly, gazing at his phone. He had his messages open and was texting Jay updates every now and then. His friend was relaying cute things their cat was doing, and that helped keep him calm.

"How bad credit card interest is. I've *told* him, he should let me pay it off. Tried to call his credit card company, too—"

"Whoa, you what?" James sat up. "I told you I didn't want you doing that."

"Of course, but I'm your mother, and it's my job to keep you from making stupid-ass decisions." The girls laughed along with her, but James's gut clenched as he sat up straighter.

"No, it isn't. I'm twenty-four, Mom. I'm dealing with the consequences. It's not like I just had a shopping spree in Montreal and then pretended I didn't owe any money. I've been paying it off for months now."

"At, what, the minimum payment? I still think you didn't need to recklessly put that on your charge—"

James unfolded his legs and stood up. She'd been against him "rushing into it" back then… never fucking listening to him in the first place. If she had, maybe she would've realized why it wasn't reckless. "My decisions what to do with my money and my body are *mine*."

Mom's eyes narrowed, and his cousins and aunt stared between them. The laughter of the characters on TV was almost jarring in the silence of the living room around them.

"Fine. I'm just saying, why pay thousands of dollars in interest when I could help?"

"Because I have a business now, Mom. I'm paying it off." He flopped back into the chair.

"Slowly."

"And," James said, his jaw clenching, "I don't appreciate you calling my credit card company. I don't want financial help from you."

He didn't mean *from you* to come out as harshly as it did, but it was true. With Mom, there'd be an obligation to recip-rocate. She'd have a string of guilt to pull when she wanted something.

His mother clicked her tongue and looked back to Jo,

forcing a smile. "And that's the opposite of what you'll be telling Kay in a few months' time. Laundry money adds up."

The atmosphere started to relax again. Leila chuckled awkwardly and twirled her hair while Jo started talking about the carwash.

James opened his messages with Ryan to scroll through the last few.

Princess movies? I'm not surprised ;) I like one or two myself...

Ryan hadn't made him feel bad about it, though. He never did, and James appreciated that.

They'd chatted a bit about that, and then Ryan had gone to soak in the tub.

As if on cue, the phone vibrated again.

You all singing kumbayah yet? I probably mangled that.

James smiled ruefully.

Far from it. Just got grilled about my debt and surgery choices... Again.

Ouch. You OK? Ryan added a heart emoticon afterward.

That made James smile even more. He didn't seem to be the type to use them, but he tried to when James did. He'd recently discovered the blushing smilie face. He used that a lot, especially when James flirted.

I'll be OK, James promised, though his heart sank. He wasn't sure about that. He added a quick, *thanks.*

Of course. I'm still picking your cute face up on Monday right?

Ryan was going to visit first thing. They could climb outdoors together before they drove back. The anticipation kept James going through this hellish weekend.

I hope so! He added the kissing smilie face, then paused and stared at it for a moment. No, it wasn't too cheesy. He sent it. Then, he added, *I'm going to sleep and hide from the interrogation. LOL. Good night.* When he got up to head to his room, nobody stopped him and he only felt relief.

Good night. Sleep tight, don't let the rudes bite. xoxo.

The sweet message helped unknot the tight coil of frustration in James's stomach as he changed for bed. Yeah, his family was rude, even if he'd grown used to it.

Why did holidays always have to end up this way?

CHAPTER
Twenty~Five

RYAN

RYAN'S HAND JUST CLOSED AROUND THE HANDLE OF HIS workshop when his phone buzzed.

It had to be James. He hadn't been texting anyone else this week. He rarely texted anyone, actually. He couldn't stop his smile as he paused on his driveway, pulling the phone out of his pocket for a glance. Then, as he scanned his screen, his smile vanished.

Half considering messaging the nearest grindr guy who can host to pick me up. Lol.

His belly was full from Thanksgiving Sunday dinner with his parents—a boring dinner compared to James's. The most exciting event in Ryan's weekend had been Ryan spilling gravy all over the beige tablecloth.

James, meanwhile, had been relaying tidbits from his last few days via text. Nothing word-for-word, and he was obviously hurting more than he was trying to let on. James had been pissed when his mom had tried to meddle with his credit card debt. Half his relatives at supper tonight had called him the wrong name and pronouns despite that hand-

some beard James had been growing in. The half who didn't
hadn't bothered correcting the first group. Then, they'd tried
to argue with him about trans celebrities. God only knew
what they'd done now.

"Shit," he murmured under his breath. The town in
southern New Brunswick where James lived was about two
hours away. It was already eight o'clock.

He'd been planning to rip through a stack of boards he'd
marked up yesterday, then fix up a few jobs James had
finished. James was learning fast, but he was still new. He'd
stopped putting the hinges on crooked, but his varnish jobs
sometimes needed a second coat.

Ryan turned to head back to the house, his thumbs flying
over the keys. Objections aside, he'd already decided what he
was going to do. As long as he had permission...

Would you let me?

James's answer was almost instant.

Hell yes. You don't have to though.

Ryan grabbed his shoes and keys, then read the message
and answered.

Good to know. Don't sign on for a couple hours.

By the time he was in the car, he had James's answer.

OK. xox.

Ryan chewed his lip. He hated James being stuck there
awaiting rescue. If he weren't so damn proud, he'd buy him a
cheap used car.

Actually, now that business was picking up, there was a
thought—he'd *need* one sooner or later. A few of their
upcoming shows were out of town. And they'd eventually get
a farmer's market stall after Christmas, or after Roger
stopped being an asshole.

The thought of adding a regular expense to the business

wasn't too nerve-racking. Hell, he could sneakily pay the whole thing off for James. Having no life and working overtime had its perks.

Now he just had to convince James to let him do it... and just this once, rescue him.

He dug through his CDs and chose his favorite mix for the road before he pulled out of his driveway.

Even though he'd strongly hinted that he was on his way, James looked shocked, and it made Ryan grin. Ryan was stiff now, but it wasn't too bad considering the drive had been dry and quiet the whole way. No stress, except the usual fear of moose.

He rolled his shoulders and unbuckled as his partner—and maybe lover—stepped out from the doorway. James walked along the low, long porch, shielding his eyes to squint through the darkness at him in the car.

"Holy shit, you didn't."

Ryan laughed and stepped out of the car while James strode down the path in socked feet. Before he could say anything in response, James was pressing up against him. James folded into his arms easily as Ryan wrapped his thin body in his own strong arms.

He always had to be careful not to crush him against his front. He didn't make the mistake of thinking James was fragile, but he didn't want to crack his back, either.

"Thanks," James murmured into his chest, and Ryan swayed on his feet for a moment. "Jesus. Where are my manners? Come on in. That's a long drive."

That didn't sound like James. It sounded like someone

near James, maybe his mom or aunt. Ryan smiled and didn't comment, though. "It wasn't bad. Everyone still up?" It was just after ten, as far as Ryan knew.

"No, most of them left, but my mom and aunt are. They're probably peeking through the curtains," James rolled his eyes.

Ryan grinned. "We can give them a show or not. Your choi—"

James's lips pressed against his as he stretched up on his tiptoes.

Ryan almost laughed with surprise. He reined in his amusement to kiss James back, rubbing his back. James felt stressed as they hugged, his shoulders hard and face finally showing his age. Normally, even not clean-shaven, James looked younger.

"Okay," James murmured after a long few seconds, and Ryan let go of him. "Come on in. I'll grab my bag and go as soon as you want."

"I'm good to turn around and drive home right away," Ryan assured him, following him up to the porch.

James wanted his family to see him kiss him. Ryan wasn't great at figuring out people's internal motivations, but he had a few guesses. Maybe James wanted to show he wasn't the ugly stepchild—understandable after this shitty weekend. Or, maybe there was something more.

Ryan didn't want to admit that he wanted it to be something more.

James opened the front door, and he was already smiling again. Ryan knew him well enough to tell when it was forced.

"Is this your friend? You should have warned us he was coming tonight." James's mother scolded him, but her tone warmed when she looked at Ryan. She had James's eyes and smile, and her hair was pinned back in a loose ponytail. She scrunched it and dusted her hands on her jeans before reaching out to shake hands. "You must be Ryan. I'm Gretchen."

"Yes, ma'am. He's my boss," Ryan grinned and shook her hand. As much as she turned on the charm, he didn't want to talk to her. "Pleasure to meet you. Sorry to show up unexpectedly."

"I'm just gonna grab my stuff." James edged for the stairs.

"You're leaving already? Tonight? Oh, it's not safe to drive at this hour." A woman who looked like Gretchen, who must have been Ryan's Aunt Kay, came in from the living room. "I'm Kay."

"Pleasure to meet you," Ryan repeated, but the moment Kay went for the teapot, he shook his head. "Oh, I couldn't. I brought lots of coffee with me. I'll be up all night if I'm not careful," he grinned.

He navigated his way through a couple minutes of the social niceties, talking about his Thanksgiving dinner and the lovely weather and how the last craft show had gone. He was relieved when James appeared downstairs, backpack on one shoulder.

"We'd better get going if we want to work tomorrow," Ryan told James, who jerked his chin in an appreciative nod.

"Of course."

Their goodbyes were quick, and frostier than Ryan had hoped. He looked away for a moment to give them privacy, then did the usual *good to meet you* small talk on the way out the door.

Those couple minutes had been fine. Nothing dramatic—no yelling, no slips in names, no snarky jokes. But, he reminded himself, the worse a person was to another in private, the nicer they were in public.

James visibly relaxed as soon as he tossed his backpack in the back seat and climbed into the passenger seat. "Thanks so much for coming down this late," he told Ryan. They pulled out of the driveway again.

Ryan double-checked his headlights as he rounded the corner. "Of course. Couldn't keep me away. You all right?"

James let out a long breath, and Ryan cast a quick sideways glance. He looked like he had sounded by text—exhausted and frustrated and wounded.

Ryan silently reached out to cover one of James's hands against his knee.

"Thanks," James murmured. "Yeah, I'm all right, I guess. Or I will be."

"Not the same thing."

James grimaced. "Yeah. I wish you could've met my dad. He's a lot cooler. But I didn't want to put him in the middle of Mom and me, and… you know. It's complicated."

"Yeah," Ryan frowned. He felt so boring—his safe middle-class family and average parents and siblings weren't a challenge at all. The worst bit was remembering everyone's birthdays.

"Sorry we're missing climbing tomorrow," James added. "I know you were looking forward to that, and me too. Outdoor climbing is totally different."

Ryan chuckled. "The rocks will still be here later."

That, at least, made James crack a grin, and then he laughed. "Yeah. I guess so."

Ryan squeezed James's hand, then let go to put both hands on the wheel. Seconds later, James slid over in the seat to rest his hand on Ryan's knee instead.

Ryan could live with this.

Once he hit the highway, they spent a good fifteen minutes comparing turkey suppers. James's sounded considerably more vegetarian, since he'd brought tofu to make his own main dish. Some of the veggie side dishes his family made sounded good.

Then, the music playing softly in the background, James let conversation lapse. Ryan was fine with that. Ryan let him enjoy the peace and quiet he hadn't had for days now. The town disappeared and endless scrubby green landscape zoomed past.

"The stars are pretty." James's voice was soft. He was leaning against the window and gazing out at the night sky.

"Yeah," Ryan had to agree. They'd only just been emerging on his way down here. Besides, his mind had been on other things, like how upset James was likely to be.

He was glad James seemed to cope well when shit hit the fan. He internalized, sure, but Ryan could help with that.

"There's a nice nature spot off the road, just outside Fredericton," James said. "The stars would look good from there."

Ryan smiled. "We'll see if we feel like stopping when we get there," he promised. "Supposed to be clear all night. By midnight it'll be gorgeous."

"Yeah," James hummed, then straightened up again. He seemed calmer again, maybe sleepy. Then, out of the blue, "I wasn't really going to message some guy on Grindr to pick me up."

"I'm glad," Ryan said. He wondered if that was the right thing to say—if James would interpret it as possessiveness. They hadn't yet discussed what *they* were. But it was true; he doubted James would feel better after going home with some random guy.

"I haven't hooked up in… three months, I think."

That was unexpected. Ryan looked over fast at James, then back at the road.

Couldn't afford not to watch the road, especially this time of night and year. A moose was so tall that its eyes were outside the headlights, so he wouldn't even see the flash in the dark. By the time you saw a moose, it was too late. He couldn't take chances even when he was alone. With James in the car, he found himself being even more cautious. But that was normal. He was always more careful with passengers, right?

"Right," Ryan said, realizing he'd been silent for several seconds now. "No luck, or just didn't want to?"

"I had offers, but…" James trailed off, then kicked his shoes off. He tucked his leg under himself, getting cozy in the passenger seat. "I don't know. Either they were gross from the beginning, or I just didn't feel chemistry. Nobody drew me in until we…"

Ryan was glad for the dark, because his cheeks were hot. James thought that about *him*? God, he could say the same. "Me, neither. I actually hadn't slept with anyone in… a little longer than you," he laughed. "I tried a rebound after my last ex and that didn't work out."

"Yeah?" James smiled. "Until I caught your eye?" He was teasing, but Ryan wanted to make him blush.

"Until you caught my eye. Bossing me around and being all smart. I like a take-charge man," Ryan grinned.

Sure enough, James was already looking embarrassed but pleased. "Cool. I never think… you know, I always assume the worst."

"Oh?"

"I figured you wouldn't be into me because of, you know.

I'm kind of my own worst enemy, but then other people are, too… so…"

"You run into that a lot?" Ryan asked. "On Grindr or whatnot?"

James nodded. "I have it in my profile now so some of them filter themselves out, but I spend—spent—so much fuckin' time answering the 101. Nobody goes and Googles it like you did."

"Least I could do," Ryan said simply. He didn't like being ignorant, after all. "And I was curious. Not in a zoo animal way…"

James chuckled, reaching out to squeeze Ryan's knee again. "Yeah, I get it."

"I just can't imagine."

"Yeah, you can," James corrected him gently. "You know what it was like growing up gay. It's not a hell of a lot different, just not as well-recognized. Most people can empathize somehow. They just go about it the wrong way. Like, if you tried to imagine being a trans woman."

"Right." Ryan couldn't wrap his head around what it would be like to be female, whether in his current body or not.

"Think of it the other way. Like, what if you looked so much like a woman that everyone around you assumed you were one? But you were still a guy, still you."

It took Ryan a minute of thoughtful silence to wrap his head around that one.

"You'd have to kind of roll with it, pretend you were one," James explained. "Since everyone's said you are, and figuring it out, let alone proving it to others, is such a pain in the ass."

"Right," Ryan nodded slowly.

"And that's not *too* far off what it's like being gay. You

know, letting people assume you're straight sometimes, just for safety or whatever. And when you tell people, that's when all hell breaks loose."

Even that said volumes. Ryan had let people assume sometimes, sure, but more for convenience than safety. Sure, there was the worksite, but his work and personal lives were separate enough. James wasn't as flamboyant as, say, Noah, but he also didn't try to swagger around or hide his glances at men.

"Right," Ryan said softly. "I've done that before. I guess I do that at work."

James nodded a little. "Roger still being an ass?"

"I haven't seen him. He's been over on the other side of the site since then. Tan's had us on separate shifts. Oh, Tan's our boss."

"Right," James nodded, drawing his leg up a little more and adjusting his seatbelt. He was sitting almost sideways, watching Ryan. "I'm glad you took the chance on me."

"You showed more business sense in a few sentences than any of my buddies who've been giving me advice for months," Ryan smiled. "And some of them are pretty smart, too."

James chuckled. "I meant on letting me work on our inventory."

Ryan frowned. James really enjoyed it that much? "You never worked with your hands before?" Oh, there was a joke there, but he wasn't going to be the crude one.

James snickered but didn't follow it up, either. "No, I have sometimes. Dad and I used to work together, before things got weird."

"Weird?"

"With the divorce, and then me growing up into a... girl,

or an attempt at one. I had to do fuckin' Girl Guides and shit," James grumbled. "Mom."

Ryan carefully avoided saying how he felt about James's mother and instead nodded. "That sounds weird."

"It was like being a... a spy," James laughed. "That's how I thought of it, to get through it. If I'd been straight, holy shit, that would've been the opportunity of a lifetime. Later on, when we were teens... some of them thought I was a lesbian and tried to hit on me."

Ryan chuckled. "I never know how to handle that."

"Me neither! Girls are fun, but I can't handle them trying to make out with me," James laughed. He was relaxed now, smiling away. "Or wanting to be my straight girl best friend. What do I do with that? Make out with random boys for their entertainment? I mean, not that I haven't... but not for a while. Not since we met. I, um, haven't wanted to."

Ryan laughed. "You're cute when you get worked up."

"Stop trying to make me blush. I know what you're doing," James teased, smacking his knee, but Ryan just laughed.

The conversation flowed easily between them as the kilometers passed.

James was in the middle of telling him about dressing in drag for a dorm party when he straightened up and looked at a road sign. "Oh, we missed the stargazing exit."

They were nearly back in Fredericton. Ryan smiled. "We can do it from my bedroom window. I've got a good horizon view. I mean, if you want..."

"Yeah. I'd like that."

Neither of them said much as they drove through the quiet suburbs toward Ryan's house. His heart thumped with nerves. It had been so fucking long since anyone stayed the night with him.

It was past midnight now. James grabbed his backpack from the seat, then lingered on the path with his hands in his pockets, his head up.

Ryan locked the car, walked up behind James, and slid his arms around his waist. He pulled the smaller man in against his front. "What do you see?" he murmured into his ear, breathing in that delicious hint of coconut.

"Cassiopeia, that W-shape up there," James said softly. The neighborhood was silent around them at this time of night. It was just the two of them, guided by thousands of stars. Ryan felt so small and so, so lucky. Of all the men in the city, the country, *he* got to listen to James's soft voice breaking the crisp, silent night air, and hold him close. James's thumb stroked his. "And there's the Little Dipper, right up there."

Ryan silently followed James's pointed finger until he made out the dish shape and handle. "Mmm."

"And that's Andromeda. The three stars together are Orion's Belt. There's his sword—"

"Or is he happy to see us?"

James almost dissolved in giggles, then elbowed Ryan. "Shush. I'm explaining."

"Sorry," Ryan grinned. He pressed a kiss against the back of James's neck. "And I'm listening."

"Good," James approved. "In the middle there? That's actually the Orion Nebula."

"I thought you couldn't see any nebulas... nebulae...? Those things, with the naked eye?" Ryan frowned, watching the little patch of light James pointed out.

"Very few, but that's one of them."

Ryan shook his head. What didn't James know a little about? If he was this smart at twenty-four, four years younger than Ryan, how much more was he going to absorb throughout his lifetime? A bit of this, a bit of that... James seemed like the Renaissance man type.

Ryan found himself hoping he was going to find out.

"Let's head in," James murmured. "I'm exhausted."

"Agreed."

James turned in his arms just enough to press a kiss to his lips, then lingered by his side as he led them upstairs to bed.

Ryan was tired from the drive and the chilly midnight air. They changed for bed together, their movements sluggish, then left the blinds open for a few more stolen glances at the night sky.

It was rarely easy for him to sleep with someone, but James was a solid sleeper. Once they found the right spots, his arm under James's head and his lips against the back of James's neck, they drifted off at the same time. James's body was relaxed in Ryan's hold, the stress from early gone as he melted into the mattress.

Ryan took one more peek beyond James at the stars that showed through the bedroom window. The streetlight outside caught the spikes of hair at the back of James's head. Finally, his eyes drifted closed.

CHAPTER
Twenty-Six

JAMES

WHAT KIND OF GUY DROVE TWO HOURS EACH WAY AT THE LAST minute to pick him up just because he was having a bad holiday weekend?

James wandered down the fixtures aisle at the hardware store. He scanned the knobs and screws and brackets for anything on sale that he could persuade Ryan to use.

That was the most romantic thing anyone had ever done for him. Sleeping together that night had been incredible, but James's worries started to sneak in. It was Wednesday, and he was already convincing himself that he'd be a terrible boyfriend.

What could he do that was that meaningful? He didn't have a car, he couldn't woo Ryan with any grand gestures like Ryan had. And as much as Ryan had made it clear that he accepted James, James kept questioning that easy acceptance. Poking at the edges, like he expected Ryan to withdraw it.

He kind of did, honestly. Ryan wouldn't be the first.

They kissed sometimes in passing—made out, even, before James redirected their time to where it was most needed: frantically finishing inventory. They had scarce hours together after Ryan was done work on the job site for the day.

During the daytime, he kept busy. He talked to shop owners downtown, or did market research. He picked up anything backpack-sized from the two hardware stores and one lumberyard he could get to by bus. He'd started bringing home smaller items—signs, especially—to paint during warm days, with the windows open and the fan on. They had to squeeze the most production time possible out of their days.

Ooh, the sale shelf had a few new items. James stopped to snap a photo, then texted it to Ryan to see if he wanted anything from it.

He was only here to pick up wall brackets for the backs of the signs he'd been painting. He'd put some paint on hold for Ryan to look at. Maybe a car *was* a smart idea... but not until the credit card was paid off.

He got a response almost instantly.

I want those 1" screws.

James bit back his laugh as he walked back down the aisle for them and texted back.

Even without assembly I can give you more than that ;)

He picked up the packet. Half off because a couple screws were missing? That was a good deal. His phone went off.

My lunch break isn't long enough for you to talk like that.

James smirked to himself. It was a confidence boost to know he got to Ryan, but they still hadn't messed around again since that first time. He was starting to wonder if Ryan was serious about this.

I'm free tonight. Oh yeah and every night bc I have no life anymore lol :)

Ryan's response was quick.

Is this Mr "we have to get ready for the show this wknd!" who won't let me make out with you for hours?

Well, that wasn't fair. It was true—they *did* have to be ready for Saturday. Before he could answer, though, James almost ran into someone.

"Oh, jeez. Sorry."

When the other guy didn't apologize in return, James was a bit offended. It had been his fault, but it was still polite to apologize back.

Oh.

Fuck. It was Roger.

The guy was a good four or five inches taller and way broader, with the kind of body that came from a lot of heavy lifting. He might have been small compared to the mountain of a man Ryan was, but James felt small against him.

And there was his brain again, reminding himself that he was never gonna be Roger's size.

James's gut twisted as Roger gave him a quick, tight smile. "Oh, hey. Ryan's partner." Roger lingered on the word *partner* in that certain way, and James reminded himself to brush it off.

"Yeah. Roger, right? Small world," James answered, his voice cool.

"Picking up stuff for your little stand? How's that going, by the way?"

Oh, that was patronizing. James worked his jaw for a second before smiling tightly again. "Our business is doing great. How's yours?"

Roger had a flatbed cart with some two-by-fours, a few half-inch rods, a stack of plastic bins, and medium brown stain. Those were the exact same supplies Ryan used for his playroom toy shelf and built-in bins. Could be a coincidence, but James suspected it wasn't.

"Fine, thanks," Roger answered, cocking his head. "Didn't expect to see you here without Ryan."

"I do the shopping sometimes," James shrugged. What was Roger doing here on a Wednesday morning? Didn't he work, too?

As if he read his mind, Roger jutted out his chin, half-daring James to ask. "The boss sent me out to pick up some stuff."

"Right." James was tempted to ask, *'For a shelf? Aren't you finishing interiors?'* He managed not to, though.

"And to get out of his and Ryan's hair, if you know what I mean," Roger grinned knowingly.

James didn't like the prickle that sent through him. "Yeah?" He knew what Roger was doing: trying to plant some seed of doubt. No doubt Roger had something against him, or maybe against Ryan. He couldn't let it get to him.

Roger wasn't taking his frosty voice as a hint. "I'm sure Ryan's told you all about him."

"Yeah." That was a lie—Ryan had just mentioned Tan in fleeting anecdotes. James was putting together all those mentions now, looking for something more. Had they once dated? Was that what Roger was so resentful about? He started strolling down the aisle toward the brackets he needed. "I gotta go, but good to see you."

"You too."

James waited until Roger pushed his cart around the end of the aisle, then let out a quick breath of annoyance. Roger never seemed to be hostile. He subtly pushed buttons, as if feeling his way toward the soft spots. One of those bullies probing to see what would hurt the most.

As far as he was concerned, secretly starting a business to steal the spot at the market had been a dick thing to do. Now it was like it was getting personal, and he didn't even know the guy. What kind of history was there between them? Or between him and Ryan and Tan?

Probably nothing, James reminded himself and headed for the checkout.

"Fucking motherfucker Jesus fuck…!"

Tears pricked at the corners of James's eyes. He'd hit his thumb for the dozenth time or more trying to get the goddamn finishing nails in. Ryan was due over at his place any time now to pick up the finished signs, and he'd barely started this last step.

He couldn't get the knack of this. Good thing the hammer was small and light. If he were hammering anything harder, he'd be black and blue now.

He bit back the sting of disappointment when he heard a knock on the door. Of course that was Ryan, and now he was setting a terrible example. For all he teased Ryan that they couldn't waste time flirting when they had work to do, he was the one who was behind.

As soon as he opened the door, Ryan stepped inside, already all business. "Hey. How's it going?"

Breathe. James straightened up and managed a quick smile. "Not great. I've been slow with the brackets."

Ryan frowned. "Yeah? You think we'll have time to cut the last batch today?"

They worked in a team, Ryan cutting out the template while James passed him pieces and tossed away the scraps.

Then they worked through the stack in much the same way to drill holes.

"No," James murmured and winced. "I need help."

Ryan looked annoyed for a second, but then he took a breath and let it go. "All right. Show me where you're going wrong."

James had never felt dumber as he pointed out the nails. "I know it's the easiest part of the whole thing, but I'm... clumsy, I guess."

Ryan puffed out a little chuckle. "Well..." He looked around at the bare apartment walls. "You don't seem to have a lot of finishing nails."

"I haven't in months," James couldn't resist commenting. The innuendo was too damn easy with him.

Ryan chuckled quickly, but he was in business mode. James's shoulders slumped in disappointment. Yeah, he'd been the one turning away Ryan's flirtation when it got too hands-on this week. But right now, he could use the stress relief.

"Right. You've only got one hammer? Pass me signs and nails and I'll do them."

"Sorry about this," James mumbled, pulling up a chair for Ryan first before finding one for himself and setting up their workstation.

"Hey, it happens."

It was such a dumb little thing—logically, James knew that. It didn't stop him feeling totally inadequate as he let Ryan do his work for him, passing over a nail at a time.

"I ran into Roger at the store today."

"Oh? Really?" Ryan looked interested now.

James bit his lip and nodded. "This morning, around ten. He sort of implied you and Tan... you know."

Ryan paused mid-hammer, his jaw dropping. "He didn't."

"Yeah."

"Tan's married."

James gave Ryan a look. He wasn't stupid enough to think that made a difference.

"Okay," Ryan conceded, "but no. He's straight." Then, he paused and looked hard at James for a second before he kept nailing in the bracket. "Are you jealous? You know he's a fucking liar. And I told you the other day—"

It was hard to explain the knot of emotion in James's chest, so he shook his head. "No, I know. I know that. I just…"

"He got to you."

"Yeah." James was quiet for a minute, trying hard not to feel like the overemotional loser here. "I think he's just jealous of you somehow. The market stall—"

"That was a coincidence," Ryan told him. "He told me he had no idea we were about to apply for it."

James looked at Ryan skeptically. Ryan was busy hammering and sliding signs, his hands moving like a well-oiled machine. "And him looking like he was going to copy your stuff."

"We all do the same kinds of products. He gets his plans from the same place as me," Ryan said.

James thought Ryan was being way too generous. Roger hadn't outright *said* anything homophobic—aside from the *partner* comment, sort of. There was just something weird about him.

"Make sure he doesn't stab you in the back somehow," was all James could say.

"What? No, he's just kind of an asshole. I think he's just

bad with people. Patronizing, lazy, and *maybe* trying to copy what I'm doing, but he hasn't tried to screw us over."

"Yet," James muttered.

"For an optimist, you're not giving him a chance."

James eyed Ryan, and this time, Ryan met his gaze. Ryan was right, but he couldn't explain the gut feeling he had whenever he saw Roger. "Fine," James relented with a sigh. "Sorry. Just, he tried to do the *oh, here without your partner* thing."

"In a gay way?"

"Kind of. A *look at you without your muscle here* way, too."

"Again... dick," Ryan conceded, "but I'll have a word with him."

"No," James waved him off. Last thing he needed was Roger thinking he needed his boyfriend involved or something. Not that he was his boyfriend, but Roger obviously thought he was. "You're right. He just happened to mention this thing he thinks you have going with your boss to me... Is that allowed?"

"Nah, but nobody would take him seriously if he reported it," Ryan laughed.

"I'm just saying. Irresponsibly, I never asked: all the levels of management know about this, right?"

"The business?" Ryan was already halfway done the stack of signs, tapping in nails in one or two blows each, and he hadn't missed one. In contrast, the backs of the signs James had done were dented. James winced and tried not to think about that. "No, just Tan does. But speaking of the hardware store, I've been thinking."

It was a clear topic change, but James let him get away with it. "About what?"

"You need your own car."

Oh, hell, yes. Well, *no*, but yes. James frowned. "Yeah. I can't get one yet, but I will as soon as possible."

Another thing he couldn't bring to this relationship—business or personal.

"I can cover it—" Ryan began, and James winced.

"In my shoes, would you let me?" James interrupted before Ryan started.

Ryan eyed him for a second, then shrugged. "Probably not if it were just friends. But we're business partners. The business can own the car."

"Right, and if Roger starts causing us problems? You know, copying our shit and selling it cheaper, driving the bottom out of the market? Or applying for shows before we do?" It sounded paranoid, but James *had* to think about it. That was his job. "Or I keep fucking up our inventory, and..." James trailed off before frustration could make him tear up like a... like a loser.

"Hey," Ryan said gently, pushing aside the finished signs and turning to James. "I won't let that happen. You're new to this, but you're doing great already."

In James's state of mind, that sounded like pity. He just rubbed his forehead, then shrugged. "Anyway, if market conditions change..."

"I can afford a second vehicle. I pay it off and I sell it. I'm not talking a new one here," Ryan shook his head.

James hated the idea of having overhead expenses yet, based on so little time in business. He leaned back and chewed his lip as he slid the next sign over to Ryan. "Maybe. We don't even have a regular market spot, though."

Something flickered in Ryan's eyes for a second as he watched James, and then he nodded. "Yeah. You're probably right."

They were quiet until they finished the signs, and then Ryan drew a breath. "Right. Off to mine to do those shelves?"

"Yep. Let me stop by the washroom and I'll be good to go."

James rubbed his face as he looked at himself in the mirror. He had fewer and fewer days where he hated who looked back at him. When they happened, it tended to be because he fucked up something that he felt like a guy *should* be able to do.

Like shop for hardware without becoming an insecure emotional wreck, pound in a couple simple nails, or let a friend help him.

And he couldn't help but remember Roger's words from the first time they'd met. He'd told Ryan it was a shame they hadn't partnered up. Every now and then, James felt like an impostor—the nebula everyone thought was a star.

There was always going to be someone out there buffer than him, better with a hammer and his hands. With more money and less time spent waiting to go from boy to man. With a bigger, better dick or a more relatable childhood.

Oh, get over yourself. There's work to be done.

As much as he knew *that* was the measure of a man, James couldn't forget that look on Ryan's face when he'd given up the car argument. He probably thought James wasn't acting much like one, and fuck it, he was right. Now, James had to prove himself all over again.

Nobody was less likely to use Ryan than James. At least, that was what Ryan told himself as he ran a stack of boards through the chop-saw, passing them off to Sam.

They were roughly finishing the kitchen today so the gas line could get installed in time. Nobody wanted to try to hunt down *those* guys if they missed their target install date. Trades weren't short in the town, but there weren't a lot of them, either.

"Three more this length, then we'll need some more nineteens," Sam told Ryan. "Roger says the homeowners want the cabinets cut back an inch," she reminded him.

"Oh, right. Gotcha."

Roger couldn't mind his own business until they were ready for him. He'd finished up next door early and had brought his annoying self over to "help" them. It made a change from him begging off to go do bullshit errands and avoid working.

He hadn't yet had a word with him about James, but he intended to. Listening to Roger all morning, he hadn't heard a bigoted word, but that didn't mean much. Ryan was reluctant to admit it, but James *was* good with people. If James thought Roger had some kind of problem with him, he could be right.

Not that Ryan wasn't worried about James. He was clearly trying to avoid committing to the business, and it was hard not to feel like he was avoiding committing to *him*. The moment this work got too hard and Ryan grew boring…

Just like Isaac, he could vanish.

"Ryan, the guys can't deliver the cabinets." That was Tan, all business as he strode up to him, a pen behind each ear and a worried look on his face. "You nearly done with that?"

"Three more boards to cut."

"Right. Then I want you and Roger to take the truck to the lumberyard and pick us up these." He handed over a list he dug out of his pocket. "And then the cabinets. Can you do that?"

Perfect. James had put a couple cans of paint on hold for Ryan to check, and Ryan hadn't gotten the chance. "Of course." Ryan didn't love being stuck with Roger at the same time, but he could get a feel for him away from everyone else, at least.

"And then I want a word with you in the office after lunch."

Ryan finished the cut and handed the board to Sam, who was holding her breath. That didn't sound good to Ryan, either, but there was no sense in worrying yet.

"Of course," Ryan agreed.

"Thanks, Ryan. Roger, did you get all that?"

Roger answered with a simple, "Yep."

"Thanks, guys."

Once Tan walked off to the house next door, Sam let out

her breath and looked over at Ryan with a questioning look. "Well?"

"Don't know," Ryan admitted. He cut the last board and handed it over, then ran his hand through his hair to get the sawdust out and snapped off his safety goggles. "Ready?" he asked Roger.

"As I'll ever be." Roger was still slow to rise to his feet and stretch. He was stiff after half an hour of sitting on the edge of the porch watching Ryan work.

"Have fun." Sam's gaze lingered on him for a moment as she gathered the boards.

She'd been watching him more lately, like she knew what was up. Ryan had been looking happier these days—his family and friends wouldn't stop telling him as much. He was out to her, and she knew he didn't like talking about his love life at work, but she clearly wanted to ask.

"We'll have to grab a beer this week," he told Sam. "I think I owe you one."

"Yeah! I've got a few things I've been meaning to ask," Sam grinned.

"About his new boyfriend?" That was Roger, blundering in as usual. He could have shouted that louder, had he *really* tried.

Sam's eyebrows rose and she glanced around, then looked at Roger. "Congratulations. I'm happy for you two." It was a neat way to shut him down.

Ryan bit back his grin of appreciation for her. "We've never been happier."

"Ha ha," Roger grumbled and strode to the truck.

Sam kept her voice down as she glanced over at him. "Is he right?"

"Something… like that," Ryan murmured back. "We're not official or anything, but…"

Sam grinned. "Good for you. About time you got back out there. Look at you—your own business, and now you're dating…"

"I know. I'm almost a grownup," Ryan grinned back at her. "See you in a bit."

"See you," Sam waved, juggling the boards to carry them inside and screw them into place.

When Ryan joined Roger in the truck he huffed with impatience, throwing off the parking brake. "Sam knows about your business, though, right?"

It's like he's trying to trick me into confessing. Ryan scrunched his eyes for a second. "Yeah, she wished me good luck before the shows last week. Oh, yeah, you haven't been around much," he added casually. "Don't worry, everyone knows."

Ryan wasn't the snarky type, but Roger was starting to grind his nerves.

"Good," Roger nodded. "You know, I'm liking this whole business thing. Long hours, though, isn't it?"

Ryan was happy to chat about entrepreneurship with Roger, swapping words about what it was like to go home and build after a long day of building.

Just when he'd nearly relaxed, though, Roger couldn't seem to help himself.

"You've got a bit of skin in the game, though, huh?"

"What?" Ryan's mind turned for a second over their low-to-zero overhead. Then, he realized what Roger meant.

"I'm not homophobic, but—"

Oh, good. I always like where this goes. Ryan tightened his jaw.

"—your James is sure… flamboyant."

"He is," Ryan agreed, smiling slightly. He wasn't going to let Roger make him say something he could run back to James with, especially since James had been rattled last time. *Your James* made him smile, though.

"Sure is the take-charge type."

"Yep."

Roger wasn't taking his hints. "Bet you like that in a partner, huh?"

"I need someone to do everything beyond manufacturing," Ryan answered. He kept his voice calm like he didn't notice the smirk on Roger's face. Roger wanted him to laugh along, and he was *not* taking the bait. "You know how much damn work just that is."

"Yeah," Roger shrugged it off carelessly. "But you can always buy stuff and resell it."

"What?"

"You know, resell."

Ryan raised his brow. "Most of the markets around here won't let you do that. Local handicraft rules."

"Suit yourself," Roger shrugged as he pulled into the lot of the lumberyard. He was still smiling oddly. Ryan started to get the uncomfortable feeling something was up besides his weird obsession with both of them. Roger, a contract employee, *had* been in the office to negotiate his next year's contract with Tan earlier that day.

That, together with Tan needing to see him, had him starting to feel mighty uncomfortable. "Look, man, if you've got a problem with my business partner or me—" he started as they strode toward the fence.

"Oh, no, not at all." Roger looked and sounded sincere, but not surprised. He'd been deliberately baiting him, then.

Ryan managed to keep the conversation terse but polite all the way through their lumberyard interactions. They loaded up the truck bed, then headed around the other side to get the cabinets and check his paint out.

"I ran into James here a couple days ago, actually," Roger spoke up.

"I'm aware."

Roger laughed and punched his shoulder in a buddy-buddy way as they headed through the aisles. "Man, what do they call them? Twinks? He sure had the eye of a couple of the guys in here…"

"Who did what now? Twinkies?" That was one of the older guys, Paul, who had been probably working there since time immemorial.

"No, twinks. Remember that guy I was talking to Wednesday? The one with the red backpack?"

"Oh, yeah. I know that one. Nice kid," Paul said, glancing under the counter. "Speaking of which, Ryan, this is for you to take a look at."

"What's that?" Roger leaned in.

God, Ryan hated how nosy he could be. "Paint," he said, which was pretty damn self-explanatory. "You got a sample?"

Paul handed over the paint stirrer. "Small world, isn't it? I knew James before he was James. My daughter was friends with him in school. Good kid. Glad he's getting his feet under him."

Ryan winced but turned the paint stick over, examining the brown stain. It was natural but rich. A bold choice, but it would work well on some of the more elegant pieces—wine bottle stands and that kind of stuff.

It looked like Roger was processing that, trying to figure out Paul's meaning. Ryan shot Paul a quick, hard glance of warning. He didn't need to say another word, though. Roger's expression had just cleared up.

"Oh, *shit*," Roger exclaimed a second later. "I didn't know he—she—" he trailed off, and Ryan's heart sank.

Instead of acknowledging Roger, Ryan hauled the paint cans across the counter. "Put these on my account, thanks. Which way are the cabinets?"

"In the back. I'll get Jon to point them out." Paul came around the counter after typing into the computer. He wasn't in a rush like Ryan.

Roger would *not* give up. "You mean James used to be…?"

"None of your business," Ryan snapped back. Even as the words left his mouth, he knew it was the wrong approach. It would only confirm what Roger was thinking.

Roger shrugged and grunted. "Not judging. Just saying, it makes more sense."

"What does?" Paul asked.

Ryan scoffed. "You've got something wrong," he said simply to Roger. "Wires got crossed," he told Paul, taking a breath to let himself cool off before he told Roger off. "Nothing important. We pulled the truck up by the second bay doors."

They grabbed the cabinets without much trouble, working together to move them. Despite his distaste for Roger, or perhaps because of it, he had incentive to focus only on maneuvering the cabinets. Once they were securely strapped into the back of the truck, he let out his breath and took the paint cans from Paul to stow behind the seat.

Ryan swung into the passenger seat after shaking hands with Paul. He'd drop them off at his car on their way back to work. Tan never minded people grabbing something quick for themselves on these outings, as long as they didn't take all day.

"Sure the paint was a good idea?"

"What?" Ryan had no idea what Roger meant, and he didn't have the energy to care.

Roger half-shrugged. "If you're in trouble for something… best behavior, all that bullshit."

"I'm not assuming I'm in trouble," Ryan answered. "But if you know what's going on, feel free to tell me."

Roger smiled and brushed it off. "Nah. All right, hopefully traffic isn't bad." He twiddled with the radio while Ryan eyed him but let it go—again. "Sorry I didn't know what to say back there, about James."

There it was. "I don't know what you're assuming out of all this," Ryan told him. "But it'd be better not to assume anything. You know what happens when you assume."

Tan loved to say it, and Roger rolled his eyes. "Ass, you, me, something like that."

"Right." Ryan folded his arms. "He's a damn good business partner. I don't know what Paul meant, but he's got a good head on his shoulders."

"Oh, he's just gay? I thought he meant…"

There's the out I need. Ryan eyed him. "You're the one who was calling James gay all day long. And yeah, if you need to know, I am. You wanna go there with me?"

"Nah," Roger said so fast it almost gave Ryan whiplash. "We're cool, man. Right?"

"We're cool," Ryan muttered, even if he didn't feel like it. He turned his eyes back to the road, trying not to act stiff. Roger switched to talking about the hockey season so far. He couldn't wait for lunch and his chat with Tan.

"I'm not allowed to do what?"

Tan looked apologetic as he sat on the desk, watching Ryan pace. "Only big projects like you're not doing, as far as I can tell. The non-compete agreement, man, I forgot all about it. Your little sideline project seems totally different."

Ryan, too, had forgotten that he'd signed one of those when he got offered work here. It was designed to keep a carpenter from moonlighting at one of the other builders around town.

"And you remembered today?"

"When I was going through Roger's papers," Tan nodded. "Since he's got his own thing going now, a lot like you." He seemed hesitant to bring it up, but he folded his arms. "Are you two competing?"

"What? No," Ryan scoffed, then sighed and dropped into a chair. "Kind of. He knew I was meeting with the manager of the North Market—heard me talking to Sam that week about it. And he snuck in there earlier to grab the spot I wanted."

Tan whistled lowly. "Is this going to be a problem?"

"Not for me," Ryan shook his head. "He's fucking himself over, man. I know he's been a no-show at at least half the markets since then." It wasn't like he'd intentionally sent spies—at least one his friends seemed to go every week and had insisted on reporting back to him. "He wasn't ready to open the doors."

Tan nodded. "I've… had word that he's been talking about you behind your back. Homophobic stuff. You know the kind."

Ryan nodded. Now, Ryan wasn't surprised. This morning he might have been. Before his chat with James, he definitely would have been. An asshole, sure, but not a *real* one: that was how he'd seen Roger before. Now he was wondering if Roger was legitimately trying to make his work life shitty. Maybe he wanted Tan to shut down his business, using the non-compete as his secret weapon.

"I hate this kind of shit," Tan huffed out a sigh, and Ryan nodded. He'd much rather just get on with his work day. "My boss wants me to deal with it now, though. Don't make me haul you both into a meeting—I told him that this morning."

"Before our honeymoon to the hardware store?"

Tan snorted. "Yeah."

Well, that obviously didn't work. Ryan wasn't going to tattle and make this shit any harder than it had to be, but he rolled his eyes.

"I've asked him to be free on Saturdays," Tan admitted. "We're going to need him on overtime. And he said he can arrange that."

Ryan nodded. "Right."

"So, between you and me, that stupid farmer's market spot might be open again soon. Now, as far as *this* job goes… I don't want bad blood."

"Right. I can be an adult," Ryan said simply, rising to his feet. "I don't care what he's saying behind my back, all right? Just let me get on with my job." He was done with the conversation, and he sensed Tan just about was, too.

Tan reached out for a quick, firm handshake and clapped his arm. "Good man. Back to it, then."

When he reached the kitchen, Ryan found Sam looking over at him as she held the cabinet in place and Roger sank screws into the wall. He shook his head and she nodded slightly, then returned her attention to the cabinets.

"All he had to tell me," he announced himself once Roger

drove the last screw in, "was that I can't build people lofts and shit. And, obviously, I can do it for me, or friends or family, just not advertise it… the non-compete thing."

"Oh," Sam laughed. "Damn."

"I know. I wanted to build lofts *on* people's lofts," Ryan scoffed, and even Roger chuckled. When Roger grinned at him, Ryan smiled back slightly.

Truce, for now.

Ryan didn't believe for a second that Roger would never make another snarky comment, but he had one big advantage: patience. As long as Roger wasn't trying to be an asshole to James, Ryan could ignore pretty much anything he said or did. One of these days, he'd fuck himself over. Ryan wasn't going to speed it up, but he also wasn't going to throw him a lifeline when it happened.

Can't keep all those balls in the air and *try to fuck me over, man.*

Roger could barely handle one thing at a time. If he let go of his grudges and stopped being allergic to hard work, he could be a damn fine woodworker. He could make a lot of money—with this company, on his own, or even both.

Or he could just burn himself to the ground. One way or the other.

CHAPTER
Twenty~Eight
JAMES

"I THOUGHT SHIT WAS GONNA GO DOWN. I DIDN'T THINK IT'D be *today*." Ryan stared at the market manager's door, then over at James. It was impossible to miss the slight smile of satisfaction on his face.

He'd refused to tell James what happened at the worksite yesterday, but James could guess. They hadn't fought—Ryan was far too calm for that—but if there were ever an excuse… Roger no doubt gave it to him.

They were walking around the market to grab breakfast and check out the competition before they grabbed the cash box from Ryan's house and drove to their craft show. James had spotted an empty table where Roger's little business should be. He'd figured they'd walk over to the office for a word with Angus.

They really shouldn't have been listening in, but it was impossible *not* to hear the raised voices.

"No, I'm not just gonna give up the table." That was Roger's voice, indignant and belligerent. "It's mine. I paid for it. I have a right to use it when I want."

"The agreement is that you come every week. Now, I don't mind you missing a week here and there, but you can't just not show up most of the time. It's not fair to our customers, and it makes us look bad. Customers want to shop. They can't do that if you're not there. And when you do show up, the table's half-empty, and the designs... aren't groundbreaking."

"I can't keep up with demand."

James looked over at Ryan, his heart twisting just slightly with sympathy for Roger.

Angus sounded calm, resigned to Roger's anger. "Other businesses can. Don't burn this bridge."

"Fine. That's fine," Roger snapped. "You wanna deal with those—"

James knew what was coming out of Roger's mouth before he even got to it, but it didn't make the word hurt any less.

"—with those *fags* from Heartwood, or Bleeding Heart, whatever the fuck they call themselves, be my guest."

James almost saw white. He grabbed Ryan's arm to march him along the outside of the building, back toward the food stalls set up around the corner.

Ryan resisted for a second before his shoulders sank. Even though Ryan had less to fear from a physical encounter, James didn't want them alone in the parking lot with the guy.

And honestly, James didn't want to know what Angus thought—if he'd say *that's not right* or just shrug and let it go.

"You all right?" That was Ryan, and James realized he hadn't let go of his arm.

James folded his arms, then nodded jerkily. He felt bad for reacting so much—he hadn't grown up with it aimed at him, after all. Similar words for girls, but they'd rolled off him as soon as he knew he wasn't one.

It was only as a teen, when he'd gone from being a tomboy to a pretty boy, that he'd ripped the band-aid off.

Ryan looked calm and steady. James breathed in his energy for a moment, then turned to lean against the building. They could talk here in semi-privacy. "Sorry. I hate hearing that shit."

"You look more upset than you were when I picked you up."

James nodded and shrugged. "I dunno. I've just had less time to get used to it."

Ryan's expression cleared up with understanding. "Ah." He hesitated for a second, looking back toward the office door, then squeezed James's arm.

The touch made James let go of the stress he was holding in his shoulders and chest. He cast Ryan a small, appreciative smile. "Guess everyone thinks we're together."

"Guess so. You mind it?"

Instantly, James shook his head. Did he mind people thinking this wonderful man was his? Hell fucking no. "You?"

"Well... *I* think..." Ryan hummed. When James straightened up with interest, Ryan pretended to think about it. "It wouldn't be so bad."

Before James could ask what exactly Ryan meant, the office door clanged open and gravel scuffed.

It was impossible to miss Roger storming down the parking lot toward them—and not just in their direction, but *for* them.

Before James could even push away from the wall and

back up, Ryan had shouldered his way between them, his body tense.

"Ryan," James hissed. He didn't want his maybe-about-to-be-boyfriend arrested, even if it was self-defense. And he didn't need protection.

Well, looking twice at Roger's clenched fists, he wasn't so sure about that.

"I know," Ryan murmured back, casting him a fleeting glance before he looked at Roger again.

"You bastard." Roger came to a stop in front of Ryan. Good. He was pissed off, but not about to throw punches, hopefully. "Lined up to take my place, no doubt."

Ryan shook his head. "I didn't do a thing, man. But I can guess what just happened."

"I just wanted a *chance*."

James resisted the urge to comment, *By fucking us over?* He wasn't going to fuel the fire if he wasn't ready to deal with the consequences.

"That sucks," Ryan said simply. "Lucky for you, you talked your way out of the non-compete, didn't you? When you were letting Tan know I had one, yesterday."

Roger didn't disagree, and James sucked in his breath. "Whatever."

"You're shitty at little stuff like this anyway," Ryan scoffed. "I don't know why you started this business, anyway, except to try to copy what I was about to do. You didn't have to rip me off."

"You calling me a bad carpenter?" Roger drew himself up to his full height—a little shorter than Ryan, but stocky.

Uh oh.

"No," Ryan said and shrugged. "You're the best damn guy

we have for interior finishings. You hire out privately on the weekends and you'll make a killing."

"Oh, fuck off," Roger snapped. He was about to shoulder past Ryan when he looked at James, then narrowed his eyes and looked him up and down.

What the fuck was that look? James stood straighter, unfolding his arms. He had no idea what Roger wanted from him.

"I think you better get to work. Tan'll be waiting for you," Ryan stated.

Roger scoffed again, then strode past them to climb into his truck. He slammed the door so hard the window rattled, and they stood where they were to watch him peel out of the parking lot.

"Jesus. He's got anger problems," James muttered.

Ryan relaxed again, stepping toward him and wrapping his arm around James's shoulders. "Yeah. You all right?"

"I should be asking you that," James shook his head. Ryan had stood up to his pissed-off coworker and competitor without once flinching.

"I'm fine," Ryan said, as if he wouldn't expect anything else. "But are you?"

"I'll be okay," James answered. "Weird moment there, but..."

"Ah. Yes. We went to the hardware store together yesterday—not by choice, believe me—and a Paul was there. The dad of one of your childhood friends."

James's gut clenched. That had to be Tiffany's dad. He was a nice enough guy, but God knew what he'd said. He just hoped it hadn't been that bad.

"He was okay," Ryan hastened to assure him. "He likes

you. But he did do the *I knew James before he was James* thing, which got Roger thinking. I think I deflected him into thinking he just meant… when you were young, but…"

James felt a little sick, but he nodded. "Right. Is that what you weren't telling me?"

"Pretty much," Ryan chuckled. His arm was a solid, reassuring weight around James's shoulders. "I didn't want to bother you."

"It's okay," James murmured. He was used to these weird, uncomfortable moments, even if they were rare now that he lived away from his hometown. "So, um, let's grab crepes for breakfast… or something healthier."

"Can you have crepes? No whipped cream?"

"I make an exception for whipped cream on *very* rare occasions."

"Oh?"

"Occasions that involve a hot guy," James drawled. He slid his arm around Ryan's waist for a few moments. They instinctively let go of each other as they rounded the corner to the food stands.

It was worth it to see the look on Ryan's face when he saw what he meant. "Oh, uh. I. That's… I mean." He was usually quiet, but now he seemed even more than usual at a loss for words.

James burst out laughing. "There's canisters of soy whipped cream, you know."

"Right." Ryan's cheeks were bright red. He strode to the crepe stand menu board and stared at it as if willing it not to whisper sexy nothings into his ear.

James's grin almost hurt his face. The only thing that made him stop grinning was approaching Angus's office door a few minutes later. They'd finished their crepes in record time.

"Hey, guys!" Angus welcomed them inside with a smile as soon as they knocked on the open door. "Perfect timing. I was about to call."

"Yeah, we ran into Roger on his way out," James muttered.

Angus winced. "Shit. Everything okay?"

"It's fine," Ryan supplied. "He yelled a bit and ran away."

That broke the air, all three of them laughing before Angus gestured at the seats. "Well, I just found myself with an empty table, and I've been getting requests to see your faces here. Apparently you're the talk of the town."

"From… customers?" James's heart raced. He hadn't expected *that*. "In a good way?"

"From customers who love, and I quote, 'that cute gay couple with the wood stuff'," Angus grinned. "Would Hartwood be interested in setting up shop here weekly?"

Ryan looked at him with wide eyes, seeking permission, and James grinned at his lover and partner. He nodded, letting Ryan answer however he wanted.

"We'd love to," Ryan answered. He shook hands firmly with Angus before James followed suit.

He's not denying it.

"Great. We'll get the papers signed now."

Crepes, a farmer's market stall, and Ryan wanting them to be seen as partners. It didn't get any better.

They were nearly at Ryan's place when Ryan finally looked at him, drumming his fingers on the wheel. "So, that's an overhead."

James knew exactly what was coming next: talking about a car again. The more he thought about it, the more he knew Ryan was right. Still, he'd let him say it. "Mmhmm?"

"You're not minding being locked into this?"

That hadn't been what James expected to hear. "Wait, what?"

"Well, you signed that contract, too. Unless you buy out of the business, you're stuck vending with me."

Stuck...? Wait.

"You thought I didn't want a car because I didn't want to be tied to the business?" James asked slowly, watching Ryan's reactions as he turned to face him better.

Ryan was watching the road again, looking sheepish. "Something like that."

Oh. Wait... "Or *you*?" James asked. Time to cut the bullshit. If Ryan wanted to be partners with him, he was gonna have to get used to a little bluntness.

"That, too."

That explained why he'd been so weird about James not wanting a car.

Goddamn. James had thought it was him being too much of a wimp to date a man like Ryan. Speaking of men who needed to speak up a little more before assuming. Ryan had something to teach James, too, it seemed.

James reached out to squeeze Ryan's knee, leaving his hand there until Ryan took a quick glance at him to acknowledge him. "I'd love to be."

"Tied to... me? Or the business?"

"Yes." James winked.

Ryan's expression softened, and he silently pulled into his driveway.

They were in the middle of the suburb, but Ryan didn't seem to care. He shut off the car, then pulled James in the second he was unbuckled.

James's knees hit the console, but he laughed against Ryan's lips as he clumsily fell into his lap. Ryan was *never* impulsive like this, and now he was hauling him in, his arms wrapping around James.

And those lips—those hot, firm lips sliding against his, Ryan's head tilting so their noses brushed. Their hands were warm on each other's cheeks. Their chests pressed together as they kissed hard, barely breathing.

James wanted this fucking show to be over *now*. He moaned softly, his chest pounding. He was hard now, rubbing himself against Ryan to grind in a few slow circles that made his whole body burn.

"I think we should head in and grab the cash box," Ryan whispered against James's lips. They were swollen and wet from their rough kisses. Every little warm breath of air sent a shiver through James's body.

"Yeah," James breathed out, easing himself out the driver's side door. He stumbled trying to climb out, but Ryan was right there behind him. Ryan slid his arm around his waist to guide him up the path toward his front door.

They didn't even make it to the couch before Ryan was pressing him up against the wall in the living room. Ryan slid a hand behind his head to cushion the impact as they stumbled together against it.

"Oh, fuck," James moaned around the sound that spilled from his throat. Ryan drew back for a split second, looking concerned. *Too fucking sweet. He thinks he bruised me.* "Tip for the future: that's the noise I make when I really want you."

Ryan lit up with amusement again, pressing up against James once more. He ground their bodies together in smooth, sinuous rolls of his hips. Those hips made wicked promises, and James's knees buckled.

James's heart felt light with joyful arousal. It was a bizarre combination—not one he could remember feeling before.

But there was no other way to describe the fact that he wanted to laugh out loud, to grab Ryan and spin with him, but also to fuck him as hard as he could handle.

"I don't know if we have time for me to fuck you the way I *really* want to," Ryan breathed out. His voice was a low rumble near James's ear. "Good and slow, until you're begging for more."

The filthy words made James's dick twitch and his thighs clench, the blood rushing to his face at the same time. His heart pounded. "I'll take a handjob for now," he laughed weakly.

"Me too," Ryan whispered. Those warm lips pressed along his neck from his shoulder up to behind his ear. "For now."

"For now," James repeated in a hoarse whisper, grinding once more against Ryan. "And, uh… if you want, we can skip condoms. You know, it's been a while, testing, blah blah. As long as you've been tested, too."

"Yeah? I have," Ryan murmured. "Skip them for everything?"

"Yeah. We'll talk when I'm less desperate for your dick in me," James laughed, and he was joined by that rich, rolling laugh he so loved to hear.

Fuck, the craft fair. They had to get a move on.

He wasted no time pressing himself against the wall, ripping the buttons open on his jeans. He slid everything— jeans, underwear, harness, packer—down to his knees. Then he grabbed Ryan by the belt loops to kiss him again before doing the same for him, until his hard cock sprang free from his jeans.

God, Ryan was hot. All hard muscles and planes in his

body. His touches were confident and hard, not delicate. James loved that. He wasn't gonna break under a little firm handling, and Ryan respected him enough to know that.

Then, Ryan's hands, firm as vices, wrapped around his thighs. James barely had time to gasp before he was off the ground, his feet groping at Ryan's waist to lock around it.

"Oh, my God, *yes*," he moaned as loud as he could as that hard cock slotted against his own. The angle took a shift or two to get right, until the base of Ryan's shaft pressed hard against and over his own throbbing cock. "I love frot. I love it so much." Fuck, he couldn't stop talking. He was that turned on.

And Ryan was silent as ever but grinning against his neck —he could just see the crinkle in his eyes.

"Shut up," James grumbled, then groaned. All Ryan's weight pressed against that point where their bodies met, against the hard veins in his shaft and against the hard nub of James's shaft.

And his hips rolled again, thrusting slowly but surely.

It was a good thing James wasn't trying to stand on his own. His whole body weakened and he squirmed with pleasure against the wall. His head rolled back as he gasped for breath.

Those lips never left him alone. The tip of Ryan's tongue trailed from the hollow at the base of his throat up his neck and throat to his jaw. Ryan bit the stubble there, then kissed down the side of his neck, finding every goddamn sensitive spot and kissing it twice.

James was almost shaking, he was so fucking turned on. Each slide of Ryan's shaft between his legs made him grunt and push forward again. Ryan's heart was pounding against his own chest. He tangled his hand in the hair at the back of Ryan's neck, whimpering again as heat flooded him just right. "L-Like that…"

Ryan thrust again. James couldn't bring himself to think of anything except the chiseled body against his, the lips kissing his ear, and the words Ryan whispered.

"—fuckin' *gorgeous.* Jesus Christ, I never knew how fucking hot this is… *you* are."

"Ryan, oh my God." The heat and pressure was almost unbearable in James's body, his legs and arms tensing. His chest heaved for breath. He was just about there, his dick throbbing in rhythm with the rest of him. His hips desperately ground forward against Ryan. "I'm com—Ryan, *yes!* Fuck!"

James couldn't manage another sound except wordless groans and grunts of pleasure. His hips shuddered and then thrust forward in quick, sharp pushes of need against that thick shaft. His limbs were weak, his weight all against the wall or in Ryan's arms, he couldn't tell which. James could barely tell up from down as climax hit him like a hurricane.

"Oh my God," James mumbled into Ryan's neck when he stopped thrusting, his muscles finally starting to relax. That hard cock was throbbing against him, and holy shit, he wanted to make Ryan feel like this. He fumbled between them, wrapping one arm hard around Ryan's shoulders.

Ryan still wasn't putting him down. He hadn't even broken a sweat at lifting him up like this. Holy shit, that kind of strength was *insanely hot.*

Ryan's cock was trapped between their stomachs, and he wasn't sure grinding would be enough—or fast enough.

"Yes," Ryan hissed when James wrapped his hand around

his shaft. Ryan's body shuddered, which was easy to feel while wrapped around him.

He jerked his hand up and down the velvety, thick weight in his hand, still pressing their bodies together and mouthing at Ryan's neck. He only kissed his way up to Ryan's ear. By then, Ryan was hissing for breath, pressing him up against the wall again, groaning his name...

And then Ryan came, nearly crushing him against the wall with his weight and passion. He pushed his hips forward, thrusting through the tight ring of James's fingers. His arms and legs shivered, but between the wall and James's hold on him, James didn't slip more than a little.

It was totally worth it just to feel every fucking *second* of that orgasm shuddering through Ryan's hard body. Ryan gasped for breath against his neck, his back arched, and his nails dug into the curves of James's ass.

James loosened his hold on his cock and stroked lightly once or twice more before letting go, well aware of the hot stickiness along him. He was a mess, and he fucking loved it.

"You can put me down," James said with a grin. He was rewarded with a breathless chuckle. Ryan carefully set him on the ground again, then leaned against the wall so heavily it looked like he was about to slide down it. "That was intense, for handjobs."

Ryan's gaze was on him again now, his lips curling into a smile. "Thanks to you, you fuckin' tease. Jesus."

James clicked his tongue, pretending to be offended. "It's not teasing when you come *that* hard."

"Fuck. The show." Ryan didn't even seem to know where to start, so James laughed and pointed him toward the bathroom. He followed after him to wipe himself down, working fast so Ryan wouldn't have to floor it to get there in time.

They were both still grinning a few minutes later. James clutched the cashbox against his legs and Ryan drove them at exactly the limit toward their destination.

"And the answer's yes on the car," James said.

If possible, Ryan's grin widened even more. "You'll let me buy one?"

"Yes," James sighed. "But we'll have a strict budget." He wasn't going to let Ryan blow their budget in a sneaky attempt to get him in a car.

The warm look Ryan shot him made his chest warm all over again. "No problem. Cheap's good. If it doesn't work out, I can pay it off that way for you."

James raised his eyebrow.

"Not to win you over or anything," Ryan said firmly, casting him a split-second glance before looking at the road. "But because money exists to make a difference."

Yeah, that was a good way of looking at it. James half-smiled. "Yeah?"

"I happened to get lucky, you happened to get... less lucky. You shouldn't have had to get saddled with all that credit card debt in the first place. I know it's not my duty or anything, but I *want* to do this. I can help make that right."

James grinned at him. "You could have just said it was for the great orgasm."

"Cheeky bastard," Ryan laughed loudly and smacked his knee backhanded. At the next red light, he leaned over for a kiss.

"That's why you lo—like me."

"Love you," Ryan corrected simply.

James felt a little dizzy for a second, the breath whooshing out of him. He drew another breath and pecked Ryan's lips. "Love you, too. Light's green. Go."

"Yes, sir," Ryan grinned and straightened up again to drive.

Twenty~Nine

RYAN

"How long *have* we been dating?"

Ryan knew the smart thing to do: redirect the question to James, and let him decide how much he wanted to tell his mother.

They'd told *his* mother the truth yesterday over tea—a week now—but James's mother was trickier.

"Depends when we define it?" James laughed and waved the question off. At least he looked relaxed, even though Ryan knew that wasn't an indication of how he was really doing.

"I never thought I'd get to meet my baby girl's boyfriend," Gretchen was enthusing. Ryan had been biting his tongue all supper. "We thought we had a gay… child. Which is okay, of course. This is all just a surprise."

James had chosen Jay's restaurant for this meeting, and Ryan could see why. At least the staff seemed to know James, so they wouldn't judge him if he snapped at his mother in public.

Now that the food was done, Ryan looked at James for

permission to answer that comment. He didn't want to tread on toes if James wasn't ready.

James just nodded slightly, his eyes hardening.

"I thought you were an only child," Ryan said to James, sipping his water.

"I am."

"Oh, no, it's just hard to get used to all this," Gretchen instantly said. She nodded, expecting him to nod along. When he didn't, she hesitated. "You know."

"No, actually," Ryan said, offering a slight smile. "I've only ever known James as James. From what I've heard, he's been James since he was a teen."

"Well, yes, but as his mother…" Gretchen trailed off.

"I don't want to step on any toes here," Ryan said, keeping his voice low. "But it hurts him when you say those things. A lot. I have to put him back together again later and remind him that the rest of the world sees who he really is. Please… for his sake, try."

She was watching him strangely, but Ryan didn't regret a word he'd said. Instead, she looked over at her son for his thoughts on it. "James?"

James blinked a couple times, and Ryan's chest tightened. Had he upset him? Fuck, he'd tried to choose the right words. "Baby?" The pet name had slipped out last week, and James had told him to keep saying it. Now it was first nature.

"I'm okay," James laughed softly, and he took Ryan's hand under the table. "I appreciate that. Yeah, Mom. He's… He's right."

"You never told me."

"I never asked you outright in so many words," James corrected her, and Ryan heard his voice wavering. He held his breath. "Didn't mean you couldn't have seen it."

Gretchen looked conflicted, but her brows were drawing down in a frown. "You don't understand how hard this is on me."

"*You* never saw how hard *you* were on me, Mom," James laughed softly. "So I guess we're even now."

Gretchen flinched. "James… I understand you're feeling defensive."

Ryan's chest was warm with pride. He didn't expect James to cut ties with his family today, or ever. At the same time, he hoped James had a little more courage to say what he had to, even if it was long overdue.

"No, Mom. You are," James told her. "And I get that. You don't know Ryan—haven't known him these last couple months. But he's right. He doesn't always say a lot, but he notices, and that's what matters to me. He sees my reactions to these things, and it… hurt that you never did."

Gretchen's jaw tightened as she looked around—maybe for the waiter. She looked like she was holding back frustration and resentment. Both of them were.

This was an intimate moment of family tension for Ryan to witness, but he couldn't imagine not being there. James was almost crushing his hand, his grip was so tight, his palm sweaty.

Ryan breathed deeply, hoping James would follow suit.

"I understand I could have made fewer mistakes," Gretchen finally answered when nobody was forthcoming. "I'm not going to change overnight."

"I never asked you to. Literally everyone else I know except you and Aunt Kay and… half of this side of the family… has seen the light. A decade later, you don't see me. Will you ever?"

"Oh, James." Gretchen tried to lean across the table, but James leaned back, and she flinched again.

"I don't want sympathy. I'm not asking to cry this out, okay? I just want to tell you what I need. If we're gonna see each other, I *need* to be who I am. I need you to stop throwing all that shit in my face like you still think it's a phase. And to stop treating it like a victory because I got a man. That doesn't prove I'm who you thought I was all along."

Ryan hadn't missed those remarks, either. He was glad James had said something, because he definitely couldn't. "Not at all," Ryan agreed, finally speaking up. "I love him, in part because he's him, but I was first drawn to him—am still drawn to him—because he's a man, and I'm gay. It's just… embarrassing for you to pretend otherwise."

"I don't understand it," James's mother finally stated, flat-out. "I don't know if I ever will."

James's cheeks were red. He drew a deep breath and let it out. "When you're ready to try, let me know." He scooted out of the booth. "I already paid. We gotta get going. Love you, Mom."

Gretchen stayed seated, looking down at the table for a moment before she met James's gaze. "I love you, too."

There was something missing between them. It wasn't that the words were empty or confrontational. It hurt much more for Ryan to witness because they both seemed to mean it.

Ryan was quiet all the way out to the new car—a cheap old station wagon. It was big enough to put down the back seats and load in lumber, but pretty good on gas, too. And, the most important factor: James liked it.

Once they were inside, he reached out to take James's hand. "I can drive."

James's eyes were wet as he glanced back at Ryan. "No, it's fine. Give me a sec."

"Of course." Ryan rubbed James's hand with his thumb, biting back the anger and frustration in his chest. It hurt to see James and know he couldn't help him. At the same time, it was a conversation they'd been needing to have.

"Thank you for saying all that."

"Of course," was all Ryan could murmur. "I can't believe they don't see you as the man I love."

After a long moment, James rubbed his eyes with his wrist, then offered him a shaky smile. "I don't want to go straight home."

"Let's head over to my buddies. They'll be done the barbecue, but not dessert. I heard Thomas baked a couple apple pies. One of them was vegan. Hopefully they didn't eat that one yet."

James gave him a shaky laugh, but a laugh nonetheless. "Apple pie sounds fucking perfect."

"Five-star rating?" Ryan teased.

James laughed again, his voice steadier as he started up the car. "I don't know yet. I'll see."

It was nice to lean back in the passenger seat and let James do the driving. For one, Ryan got to see a bit more of the town he usually overlooked while driving. And he got to put his hand on James's knee in moments like these and watch his bright spirit unfurl again, one smile or joke at a time.

———

"God, moms can be terrible," Floyd frowned with a quick glance at Greyson. Behind him, Jackson nodded solemnly.

"Yeah," James sighed. He'd just recounted the whole story. Ryan had never been more grateful to his friends for listening and getting it. "My family could accept me being gay, but not trans. Apparently that's a step too far."

"On the bright side," Cam spoke up, handing over a beer, "we have a dozen more of these."

That lifted the mood enough for James to laugh, and the rest of them chuckled, too.

"Also, a guest suite if you two wanna stay here for Christmas."

Thomas nodded. "We can let Santa know to expect two more."

Whoa. Even Ryan just about fell off his perch on the footstool near the chair James had claimed. "Wh-What?" They hadn't hinted that this invitation was coming.

"Assuming you don't make plans with your parents," Noah nodded at him. "We're probably all gonna have a little thing on Christmas Eve here, together. Then Christmas Day, I know Cam's parents—the Riley parents—want to see them and us. They invited anyone else we want to come along. Floyd, your parents are seeing you two, right?"

"Yeah, and Kevin and Matty will be in town, but their parents wanna see them, etc, etc," Jackson waved his hand. "But the point is, Christmas Eve together here. You can come along to our parents if your parents aren't around for Christmas, Ryan."

Ryan's chest was warm with the invitation. He jerked his chin in a quick nod. From how readily his mother had taken to his new boyfriend, they'd kill him if he snuck off to the

Rileys' for the holiday, but the offer meant a lot to him. And, he suspected, even more to James.

"Thanks," James nodded. Ryan knew that look on his face —trying to keep it cool.

"And any other holiday," Chase added. "They've been more than kind to me, since I don't… exactly have anyone else either."

James looked startled as he glanced over to Chase. He hadn't been around when Chase's family tried to chase him down and beat the Bible back into him, but Ryan remembered it well. "Oh. Shit. I'm sorry."

"No, it's okay," Chase smiled slightly.

"And his mom's not exactly a barrel of fun," Floyd jerked his chin at Greyson, rubbing his arms. "But we make sure everyone's got a place for holiday dinners that are way less shitty than ever before."

"Can't promise there won't be bad jokes and really awful cranberry sauce," Alex shook his head.

Thomas gasped, straightening up and pointing his bottle at Alex. "You said you liked my cranberry sauce!"

It was an undertone, but everyone heard it from Jackson as he rose to his feet. "*Ohshit.*"

Even Thomas laughed. "We're having that out later," he informed Alex and looked back at James. "My cranberry sauce is just fine."

"No doubt it is," James agreed solemnly, then cracked up with the rest of them.

Ryan scooted his footstool back a little until he was beside James's chair. He wrapped an arm around James as conversation drifted to what tofu turkey tasted like. When he rubbed James's back, James's eyes nearly closed and he leaned into him.

Not an ounce of tension there.

James was starting to realize what Ryan was determined to ensure: no matter how things went with his family, everything was going to be okay for him.

Not just for him… for both of them, together.

"Love you," James whispered, so softly it was for Ryan's ears alone.

Ryan pressed his lips into James's hair and echoed the words. He let himself get lost in the moment before they realized someone was trying to talk to them.

"And our last set of lovebirds over here have no opinion on stuffing. Well, I'm sure they do, but…" Noah clicked his tongue innocently.

Though he blushed, Ryan was grinning, too. "I like it. James?"

"Mmhmm."

As conversation turned to hockey, politics, and local festivals, Ryan shifted to share the chair with James. He was happy just to have his arm around James for hours on end. It was James who had to finally suggest they get going before it was too late.

The look in James's eyes as they headed for the car made a little shiver run down Ryan's spine. In the last week, since that frantic encounter against the wall, they'd made out more than ever before. They hadn't had a spare evening without the business interrupting them.

Not until now.

"You don't have to be in *too* early, do you?"

"Nope," Ryan confirmed. Even if he had, he wouldn't have cared.

"Perfect," James smiled. "I'll bring you home, then."

"Sounds like a plan."

CHAPTER
Thirty

JAMES

"Oh, man. I can't believe we ever thought we should keep business and romance separate." James grinned at Ryan as he held the door for him, then kicked off his shoes. "That was a terrible idea."

Ryan laughed. "It's a good idea. Just not for us."

"Shh. I don't want to hear sense."

Ryan pretended to zip his lips, and James laughed. Once their coats and shoes were off, he approached Ryan and slid his arms around his waist, stretching up onto his tiptoes to kiss him.

"So, was that pie a five-star rating?" Ryan grinned, pecking his lips.

James clicked his tongue. "Definitely. You know what else is?"

"Mmm?" Ryan's grin grew. It was hard to kiss him when he was grinning, so James scowled at him until he relented. "Sorry."

"Better." James kissed his lower lip, then gently sucked it

between his own and flicked his tongue along it. "I was going to say your friends are."

"Our friends," Ryan corrected, smiling warmly at him.

James smiled even more. All the guys had been completely chill with him from the beginning, and that was rare in a group this size.

Not all of them were touchy-feely—Chase, Noah, Thomas, and maybe Greyson had listened to his story about his mom closely. All of them looked the most sympathetic. The others didn't wear their hearts on their sleeves quite so freely. He could tell they didn't want him crying on their shoulders or anything. But they'd passed him the beer and told jokes to cheer him up, and that counted for just as much.

Welcoming him into their holiday meals was really sweet. His dad was going to be away, and he didn't want to see his mom without Ryan around for the time being. He hadn't known how to bring that up with Ryan, but they'd saved him the awkwardness.

"Our friends," James agreed, swaying on his feet with Ryan for a moment. "Let's lie down."

"Mmhmm." Ryan steered him toward the bedroom with his arm firmly around James's waist. James resisted the urge to lean into him too heavily.

He loved it when Ryan pushed him around a little—especially when that meant lifting him off the ground, like last weekend.

Christ, that had been the hottest thing ever.

That thought led him to another: they finally had an evening together, and every time they brushed, there was still that spark of chemistry.

The moment they collapsed together on the bed, Ryan

pulled James in against him, then on top of him. Ryan's hand gently ran down his back to rest in the small of his back. James braced himself with his arms above Ryan's head and kissed him.

Even making out with Ryan was fucking hot. He kissed slow and dirty, with tongue, and touched James while he did it. His hands were always wandering up James's sides, his fingers trailing along his ribs or up his spine, or rubbing James's chest, cupping his cheeks, touching his hair…

Everywhere Ryan touched, James's skin tingled with pleasure. "I think we never got around to what you were promising me," James murmured. His back rippled as Ryan cupped the back of his neck.

"I think you're right."

"We should fix that," James grinned.

Ryan nipped his lip. "Mmmm. Does that mean I get to undress you?"

"Oh, yeah," James laughed, raising his hands as Ryan peeled his collared plaid shirt off, then his t-shirt. By the time Ryan's hands fell to his waistband, he was already prickling with pleasure and heat. He had to resist the urge to shove his lover's hands away so he could do it faster.

"This would be easier if I just had you…" Ryan grabbed his hip and shoulder. They flipped over, James's head in the pillows as Ryan blanketed him.

James laughed with surprise and squirmed. "Probably." He kicked his legs when Ryan stripped his jeans off, then moaned. Ryan's hands slowly ran up his shins, over his knees, up his thighs.

"I love your body hair," Ryan murmured. "And your stubble. And your treasure trail…" He leaned down to kiss the inside of James's thigh. "And that cock. It's intriguing."

"How so?" James grinned, biting his lip as Ryan stripped off his boxers.

Ryan wrapped his hand around the shaft, stroking his hand to the base and grinding it into James's body to rub his cock under it. He'd got the knack of it almost instantly. James couldn't overstate how much he appreciated that.

"Fuck," James breathed out, almost forgetting his own question.

"Because I wonder what it'd feel like to have you take charge," Ryan grinned.

James shivered. "Oh, God, yeah. Say the word. But next time."

"Next time?" Ryan laughed.

"Goddamn it, Ryan," James sighed dramatically. "I have been waiting to get your cock in me since you hit on me at that art auction. I am *not* going to let you get away."

Ryan's laugh rolled around the bedroom, his hands pausing for a second as he shrugged off his shirt and tossed it aside. "All right. As you wish."

Christ, that barrel chest, the muscles rippling from his shoulders down to his wrists, and lining every inch of his torso… His pecs, especially. They were so kissable.

James stared hungrily, not even making it subtle. He loved Ryan's body, and he wanted it on him.

"So, do we need a condom, or…?"

James grinned. "No. My doctors say pregnancy's really unlikely unless I stop T for a while."

"Oh." Ryan grinned. "Cool. So you don't mind."

"I want to try without it," James said. "I haven't before."

"Never?"

James shook his head. He watched Ryan yank his jeans

and underwear off, bracing himself, until he was naked. God, he was distractingly hot. "Didn't want the risk."

"I get it. I only did with… my last ex," Ryan murmured. "If you want to, I do." Ryan pressed a quick kiss to his lips.

James braced his feet and buckled against Ryan, pulling his harness down and off. He was *so* going to take Ryan up on his confession of curiosity later, but for now…

"And, uh, which…?"

James laughed at Ryan's expression as he furrowed his brow, trying to figure out how to ask the question. "Either. Let's start with what you're used to."

"Deal," Ryan murmured, pressing his lips against James's again. His body blanketed James's. He was grinding down in that slow, sensual rhythm, his cock rubbing James's. They both hardened with arousal. Just having warm skin on skin, Ryan's lips trailing along his jaw, was enough.

"I can feel you getting hard," Ryan breathed out, his eyes wide. "Fuck."

"Hot?" James teased.

"Fucking hot," Ryan agreed.

James smirked. He reached between them to drag Ryan's hand to his dick. He guided him into pinching it between two fingers and a thumb. He bucked his hips into the touch while he wrapped his hand around Ryan's cock. "Nnh, like that."

They stroked each other slowly at first, exchanging long, slow open-mouthed kisses. Ryan's other hand cupped his cheek, then ran down his chest to tweak his nipples.

The electric jolts that ran through his body were hard to explain. Ryan had figured out exactly how to play with them to get him to react. He moaned with pleasure through their kiss. "Speaking of a tease."

"It's not a tease if you come afterward," Ryan whispered against his lips with a wicked smile. He tightened his grip on James's cock and tugged a few more times before he let go.

"Fffuck," James whispered, his lips catching on his lower lip as he tried to catch his breath. "You're a bad man." He ran his thumb over the tip of Ryan's hard cock, then stroked his hand down the thick shaft. "Lube's over there."

"Terrible," Ryan agreed. He grabbed it and grinned, squirting it across his fingers.

James spread his legs, then gasped when wet fingers slid inside him. It made his skin prickle with pleasure, the hair standing on the back of his neck. "Oh, *fuck*."

"You all right?"

"Impatient, but yeah," James retorted.

Ryan chuckled deeply and crooked his fingers inside him, pushing his fingers inside a few more times before he pulled them out.

"Nnh. For future reference, it still feels good to me, even if I don't have a prostate," James grinned.

"Noted," Ryan murmured.

James pulled him in for a long, slow kiss before wrapping his legs around his waist. The thick warmth pressing against him, then into him, made him shiver with pleasure.

Ryan echoed his groan, kissing him a couple times as he slid gradually in, inch by inch. He pulled his hips back for a quick thrust or two.

"Oh, fuck, yes." James's heart pounded at the feeling. Not quite like anything he'd felt before. More intimate than before, not because they were bareback, but because it was *Ryan* inside him.

The thought made his skin prickle all over again—or maybe that was the next thrust of Ryan's hips as his hardened hand closed around James's hip. He braced himself on his elbows and knees.

James moaned his encouragement and kissed Ryan hard. He wanted to tempt him to speed up his pace as he thrust their bodies together. Ryan's cheeks were red, his hair wild, his eyes utterly attentive to James's every facial expression.

Best of all was that thick cock plunging into him, and the scrape of his own cock against Ryan's washboard stomach. His foreskin dulled sensation enough to tease the crap out of him. Being stretched and filled for the first time in so fucking long was beyond comparison.

He was gonna have to schedule time for sex now, wasn't he?

Ryan was out of breath and moaning into his mouth. James had the distinct feeling he wasn't going to be far behind. He squirmed until he got a hand around his own thigh and between them, jerking himself hard as Ryan pushed into him.

The bed thumped against the wall with each lurch of their bodies, James's head slipping off the pillows. Ryan just kissed him harder and teased his nipple by circling his finger around it. James's whole body burned with pure, simple *need*.

"I'm gonna come," James whimpered when he felt his body drawing tight. Pleasure jolted through him, and his body tightened involuntarily around that thick cock inside him. He tightened his fingers around himself and groaned when he felt a fingertip brushing over a nipple. Ryan's lips slid along his open mouth as his tongue teased the tip of James's.

James's whole body shuddered, tightening until he couldn't breathe. He came in a wave of white-hot pleasure that ripped a cry from his throat. "Yes! Ryan! Ohhhh," he groaned, his chest heaving as he bucked against Ryan's solid body. Their chests rubbed as he clenched around that hard cock, squeezing his eyes shut.

It was like nothing else when he felt Ryan coming, too—inside him, even as he clenched and shuddered and thrust up into his own hand.

"Ohhhh, *yes*," Ryan growled in his ear, thrusting hard and burying himself deep inside with each squirt and shudder of his cock. His expression was taut with pleasure, that hard body rippling and clenching all around, over, and in him.

Sweaty and kissed to heaven and back, James felt wet all over in the best fuckin' ways as Ryan slid out of him.

"Oh my God, that was the best sex of my life," James moaned. He didn't feel shy about admitting it.

Ryan grinned and mouthed at his jaw, even though his eyes were hazy and his body still twitched and shivered. "Me, too, baby."

James loved the nickname. He rubbed Ryan's back as he dropped his feet to the mattress again, then hauled him in to hug him as hard as he could.

Ryan rolled onto his side and tucked James against his front, grabbing the pillows for them to be a little more comfortable. Then, James closed his eyes and let Ryan kiss him slowly, over and over, until their bodies cooled.

James's chest was impossibly warm. He'd always thought it was dumb to say things like this in the heat of the moment, but suddenly, he understood why people did it.

He couldn't wait a single second to tell Ryan. "I really love you."

He opened his eyes to peek at Ryan's response.

Ryan was smiling, his eyes half-open, his finger lightly

brushing down Ryan's side from shoulder to hip. "I love you, too, James. Like I said before… I'm glad I chose you."

"As your business partner, or as your boyfriend?" James smiled, running his hand up to Ryan's cheek to peck his lips again.

Ryan pressed his lips against the tip of James's nose, then his forehead. He whispered, "Yes."

As his energy drained away, his eyelids sliding closed, Ryan's body was warm under his hands. James's nose was filled with the scent of him, his lips tasted of him, and Ryan's deep breaths broke the contented silence.

James was the luckiest man alive.

TWO MONTHS LATER

"Do you want more punch?"

James giggled as he leaned into Ryan's side, his eyes half-closed. "I think I'm good on punch," he assured his boyfriend.

The sheer curtains were pulled across the sliding glass doors that formed a walkout from Cam and Noah's guest suite to the shared backyard. It was easy to imagine the dark night and gently-drifting snow outside, though. Christmas had come with snow, as usual, and the only reason James didn't mind it was because he didn't have to go outside in it.

That, and it was kind of romantic in moments like this.

Christmas Eve had been one of the best in his life. All of their friends—even Kevin and Matty, whom he'd met in person for the first time when they flew in from Toronto yesterday—had gathered at Cam's place. They'd swapped gifts, drank a lot of beer, and watched Christmas movies until midnight.

And then Jackson had got down on one knee by the Christmas tree, "found" one more present under it, and proposed to Chase. Chase cried as he said yes, the rest of them whooping and hollering with surprise and delight. Jackson hadn't breathed a word of his intentions to any of them beforehand. Alex had dropped a few hints that he'd been thinking about it himself lately. Apparently, they'd all have to keep waiting for that moment.

After celebrating *that*, they'd all made their way home. Floyd and Greyson went back to their place, Kevin and Matty to a hotel despite the offer of a guest room in one of their houses. Ryan and James came here, to the guest suite in Cam's house.

"I almost forgot this is my first Christmas away from my parents," James admitted at last, resting his head on Ryan's shoulder.

"Mm?" Ryan murmured. "Well, we're off to mine tomorrow."

"I know," James assured him with a chuckle. Ryan was no doubt worried about him, especially after hearing that. "It's fine, though. It's bittersweet, but it's… it's okay."

Ryan had liked his dad from the moment they were introduced. They didn't see him, or Anna, as much as they'd like, but James wasn't alone. With the Rileys having his back, he never would be. Plus, Ryan's parents were nice. Boring, Ryan always said, but James liked them.

Things had been hard with his mom's side of the family. They might get better—he didn't know yet. Ryan had had his own trouble at work with Roger being a dick now and then. It didn't bother the unflappable man, and Tan was firmly on his side, so Roger had let it go. James trusted that somehow, things would work out for the best. With his credit card paid off, James was less stressed about everything.

He pressed his lips into Ryan's shoulder, and Ryan squeezed him into his side.

"I'm glad you're doing okay," Ryan murmured. "Shall we get to bed? We have a lot of Christmas dinner to eat tomorrow."

"And gifts to open, and snow angels to make..." James teased.

"I'm not making snow angels."

James giggled. "What if I push you into the snow and make them around you?" He pulled back the covers, tucking himself against Ryan's front and letting Ryan drape his arm around him to pull him close.

"We'll see," Ryan grunted.

James was totally gonna make him make snow angels.

As he closed his eyes, his heart glowed with joy. Everything was perfect: the scents of wood fire, sugar cookies, and pine; the warm weight of a strong arm around his chest; but most of all, the sound of Ryan's steady breathing beside him.

"Merry Christmas, Ryan," James whispered.

He thought Ryan was asleep, but he heard a sleepy chuckle from behind him. Ryan's arm tightened for a moment. "Merry Christmas, love."

He didn't have all the answers, but he didn't have to have them yet. Neither did Ryan, or any of these Rileys who had taken him in—both blood-related and those bonded by love and friendship.

Together, they could live, love, and be happy. No matter what had happened yesterday, today could always bring a smile, and tomorrow would always be a bright, new, beautiful day.

Flaunt (F-Word #1)

"I'M AFRAID I'M TOO MUCH FOR HIM."

Nic had no choice but to be himself. The programmer escaped his family and moved to LA for a fresh start when he transitioned. When he runs into the force of nature called Kyle—green hair, garters, and all—Nic is pulled headlong into the center of his world… he's just not sure he belongs there.

Loud, loving, and unapologetic, Kyle works day and night at his charity and spends the rest of his precious time with his co-parented son. Flings are one thing, but Nic makes Kyle want to hold him forever. And when the chips are down, Nic shows up.

They've spent years avoiding the very thing they're yearning for. But in each other's arms, they finally feel loved, safe—even free. Can two men who feel like they're not enough and too much find something just right?

Flaunt is the first book in the F-Word series, which features queer found families, characters choosing their own labels, a lot of trans joy, opposites attracting, spice for days, and the happily-ever-afters we all deserve. This novel can be read as a standalone.

About the Author

E. Davies writes feel-good, low-angst romance that never fades to black when the going gets good! Born in Canada, after 16 moves and counting, Ed has finally put down roots in north London.

He emerges from his writing nest to coo over fuzzy animals, flee from cute guys, dance through the streets with his chosen family, put together fierce looks, and—most of all —befriend local flowers.

You can find all available titles at: www.edaviesbooks.com

FOLLOW E. DAVIES ONLINE:

- amazon.com/author/edavies
- bookbub.com/authors/e-davies
- facebook.com/edaviesauthor
- goodreads.com/edavies
- instagram.com/edaviesauthor
- x.com/edaviesauthor

Also by E. Davies

Sunrise Island Brothers:

Collide

Stranded

Hart's Bay:

Hard Hart

Changed Hart

Wild Hart

Stolen Hart

Significant Brothers:

Splinter

Grasp

Slick

Trace

Clutch

Tremble

Riley Brothers:

Buzz

Clang

Swish

Crunch

Slam

Grind

Brooklyn Boys:

Electric Sunshine

Live Wire

Boiling Point

F-Word:

Flaunt

Freak

Faux

Forever

Freedom

After:

Afterburn

Afterglow

Aftermath

Shared Universes:

Shelter

Adore

Miracle

Redemption

Limelight

Barely Regal

www.ingramcontent.com/pod-product-compliance
Lightning Source LLC
Chambersburg PA
CBHW050838190726
48286CB00007B/2134